Walking In the Graveyard

Dixie Jo Jarchow

Published by Wintergreen Books, 2024.

WALKING IN THE GRAVEYARD

First edition. February 19, 2024.

Copyright © 2024 Dixie Jo Jarchow.

ISBN: 979-8224620098

Written by Dixie Jo Jarchow.

Also by Dixie Jo Jarchow

The Hunt for Mel's Gold
Hades' Redemption
Huntress Moon
The Gingerbread Man
Walking In the Graveyard

Watch for more at dixiejojarchow.com.

Table of Contents

Duality of Dreams 1

Overwatch 10

The Kiss 11

The Wave 15

The interview 19

The Natural Leader 26

Last Dance 31

The Moon Trees 35

The Timebomb 40

Urban Horror 52

Chickens don't do it for me. 56

Jazz Man 59

Black Gold 61

Greener Pastures 65

Deja vu 70

Freedom morning 73

Making a Difference 76

The Interview 80

To my fellow creepy writers.

Duality of Dreams

Probably my all time favorite story. Makes me cry when I read it, even now. DJ

Mr. Cusar droned on discussing integers as if they were the most important thing in the world. Amber yawned, mouth wide and unashamed. The classroom was baking hot as the last days of school dragged on. The sun warmed her long brown hair and she used it as a curtain to shield her nap.

Amber propped her head on her hand to support the illusion she was studying her math text and drifted off to imagine her graduation party. Shari was having a deejay at her party and wondered if her parents might spring for one. "Par-Tee! Par-Tee!" She chanted in her mind as she dozed.

###

The cell was old concrete, crumbling and crusted in the high desert air. A whim of a breeze floated up the warm dust, coating everything. Mark woke, suffocating in the dry heat, chained to an iron circle in the floor. Christ, this was the real thing. Everything hurt.

Voices filtered through the hallway to his cell. Was Jerry alive? Jerry, his pilot, experienced, ultra-cool with that shock of white hair he'd had since he was in his teens.

Even as their helicopter fell from the sky with engine failure, he was cool, trying to save it; save them. He had an image of Jerry's face as they pulled him out of the wreckage. Shit, he was dead. A tear tracked down his dusty face until it was absorbed in the grime.

This sector was supposed to be cleared, but was anywhere in Afghanistan really safe? They hadn't been in the air more than a half hour before they crashed. Help might be just over the next rise, but the terrain was so mountainous that no one would realize he was here. Crappy mountainous shit.

The door to his cell cracked open and he had his first view of his captors. His chest tightened and he took a deep breath. Kids! No more than teens. Three dirty boys looked at him with huge, dead eyes, rifles slung over their thin shoulders.

He smiled at them through cracked lips. As if on cue, they moved into the cell. The tallest swung his rifle in a wide arc. Mark tried to get his head out of the way. Pain crashed into his shoulder and then the beating began for real.

They stood around him kicking and swinging their rifles. Each kick forced air into his bruised lungs. Things broke away inside of him. Grunting at first, he yelled through clenched teeth, relaxed his jaw after a tooth chipped. He swallowed dry dust and screamed as the beating continued forever.

She screamed as she lurched from her seat and knocked Nate What's-His-Name out of his desk. Part of her brain noted his shocked, angry face as she struggled towards the door. She knocked into the door in her urgency and clenched her teeth so hard a tooth chipped. She swallowed dry dust as her track speed kick in. She flew down the hall until she realized she wasn't in a cell, wasn't being beaten.

She stopped at the first drinking fountain and drank until she gagged. What the heck was that dream? So real. She was screwed. First, she'd hit the office and explain. Then, she'd have to apologize to Cusar. He wasn't really that awful but he'd hate her guts after this. Only two more days of school and then it wouldn't matter anyway.

Walking towards the office, she concocted her story. She'd had a dream in class. Simple as that.

Amber never had a dream so vivid. Her hands shook as she opened the door and she took a deep breath before she entered.

She told her parents as soon as they got home, knowing they had gotten a call from the school. They were so nice about it. Could have happened to anyone, they said. She endured their fables from back in the day.

She said her prayers that night; something she hadn't done in forever. Threw in a prayer for Mark and slept.

He moved back to gauge the length of the chain, the give of it and a coughing fit took him. He wiped his mouth with his shirt tail and saw the shock of blood on it. His ribs were most likely broken. The coughing continued and he gasped for breath. He had to get out of here before they killed him.

The racking coughs woke Amber. She gasped for breath. She had to get out of here. She flew out of her bedroom, ending up in the kitchen. The clock on the stove said three a.m.

No way was she going back to bed for more of those tangled dreams. She turned on the computer and searched for downed helicopters in Afghanistan.

"Honey, are you ok?" Her mother stood in the doorway, t-shirt and sweatpants.

"Mom, there was a helicopter lost in Afghanistan yesterday. Two men missing." She pointed to the screen.

Her mom glanced at the display. Worry fringed her eyes.

"You saw this and it caused your dream."

"I don't ever look at the news. One of these guys is alive. We have to tell someone."

"I'm sure they're looking for him."

"But I know where he is."

"Where is that?"

"A cell."

"What can you do? You aren't even sure it's real. Let's talk after school tomorrow. Go to bed, dear."

Her mother was right; she couldn't help anyone. She prayed not to dream.

In the morning, she rushed downstairs and accessed the army website. It was focused on recruiting but they had a discussion board. She plugged in her question with delicate fingers.

"Mark crashed in a helicopter with Jerry. Jerry has a white streak in his hair and was the pilot. Mark is in a cell, chained to a ring in the floor and three teenage boys with rifles are beating him. I dreamed this. It was so real. Can anyone confirm any of this? Amber"

She got ready and her mom drove her to school early to apologize to Mr. Cusar. The last day of school was finally here. She told her story so many times that when class began, even the guy she knocked out of his seat was okay with her. She made a point to smile at her lap as if embarrassed.

The summons to the office came five minutes before the bell. She did one big fist pump as she walked. Someone read her email.

In the principal's office, her mom sat stiff-back in a chair wearing a look that told her this wasn't over by a long shot. The principal, an older man shuffled the papers on his desk as if he'd rather be anywhere than here. An army guy, pressed uniform with a ton of medals, stood at attention behind an older man.

The older guy wore a battered suit with cigarette stains on his index finger. He gestured for Amber to sit beside her mother. His age was hard to guess. His hair was short but not shaved like the soldier behind him. He wore wire-rimmed glasses.

"We saw on a message board that you had a dream," His voice was low and smooth and Amber smiled.

"It was a weird dream, very vivid, not like a usual dream. His helicopter crashed and he is in a concrete cell. Three teenage boys were kicking and beating him with rifles. He doesn't think Jerry's alive but Jerry has this white streak in his hair and he was the pilot. They were in Afghanistan but I don't know where." It rushed out as one long sentence.

"Is there anything you didn't put in your message?" He leaned in to hear her answer.

"No. I hope he's okay. You're looking for him, aren't you?"

"Do you know anyone in the military, Amber?"

"No." It was as if they were alone in the room, just the two of them.

"Is there a website you're getting this information from?"

"No, it's my dream!" He didn't believe her. "You have to find him." She could hear the shriek in her voice and took a deep breath.

"We will. In the meantime, if you get any other information, call me at this number." The plain white card was thick, marred only by the deep impression of a phone number. He nodded at the principal and her mother, then left.

Her mother glared at her briefly, then gave her a hug.

The principal let her go back to class.

What she really should do was go somewhere and sleep, but she had something to do first. Today was the end of the year celebration at school and, as a senior; she had some butt-kicking to do.

She was going to run the mile with all the seniors on the track team and whatever teachers manned up. She was the fastest senior and would win easily except for Mr. Bowser, a social sciences teacher. He was just out of college and still ran 50 miles a week. He cranked out marathon times under three hours. His blinding speed would kill her in the mile but she could cruise past everyone else. The two senior guys were no match for her.

She'd been looking forward to this since sophomore year when Mr. Bowser told her she could develop some speed, if she trained.

The celebrations of the last day blurred by her. The mile was the last event of the day. Mr. Bowser lined up after the two boys and Amber. She nodded thanks but it crushed her that he would run with them for a while and then hit the afterburners.

The gun crack startled her and she took off. She knew she had to stay close to Bowser and surged past the other runners to stay with him. Bowser had run a 4:01 mile in college and he was stronger now.

On the second lap, Bowser slowly pulled away. She forced her head up and surged after him, leaving the two boys and the rest of the girls behind. It was suicide to try and stick with him. She risked burning out and finishing last if she used up all her energy this early in the race.

The boy soldiers stomped on his hand when they came back the second time. They laughed about it, satisfied for the moment and left him. He was afraid they were working up their nerve to kill him.

A blessing in disguise, his mangled hand slid through the manacle around his wrist. He stood and slid the door open. A quick look and he moved quietly through the hallway. Where were they? He smelled smoke and then he heard them chattering and headed the opposite way.

He was in a squat bunker, only a few low rooms. Another step and he was outside in the baking sun, figuring which way to go. His ribs hurt and his hand throbbed but he started off in a ragged jog back towards what he thought was the direction of the crash site.

The crack startled him into a run. They were shooting at him. How far could he go, dehydrated and hurt? He upped his jog to a stumbling run. When he was in high school, he was on the track team. Helluva time to think of that now. He imagined he was running the mile of his life.

###

The dust rose around Amber and she pounded down the trail, Bowser forgotten. She lengthened her stride and changed her breathing to one breath per stride to get the needed oxygen. Grime rimmed her mouth and dust filled her throat, but she willed herself to continue. She was dehydrated and her hand hurt, her ribs were on fire but she pumped her arms and ran faster.

#

The terrain was rocky and uneven, with a slippery coat of dust over everything. Mark tried to remember where this was in relation to the nearest troops. He flashed on his view from the helicopter and the tents just before they crashed.

Blessed God, let it be this way. His stride faltered when he hit an uneven patch. He rounded a small rise and saw the U.S. Army tents a half mile away, a mirage of safety, they shimmered in the heat. He would never make it. Chest burning, coughing blood, he would die here. The sound of running feet echoed behind him.

###

She passed Bowser without realizing it, the sound of running feet echoed behind her. She found another gear and pushed herself through it. Her stride faltered, chest burning, she coughed with the effort of getting enough oxygen for both of them. Less than half a mile to go and the finish shimmered with the heat of the track. She increased her pace and gritted her teeth.

She dug deep and exploded in a final kick. Lungs burning, her chest on fire, she willed herself faster.

She felt him stumble and begin to give up; swallowed in pain.

"We will make it," she told him. He nodded and took strength from her, began pumping his arms in sync with her. They matched stride and she brought him with her, past the screaming crowds, ignoring any pain until they collapsed together at the finish.

Overwatch

I don't often write poetry but here and there I grasp at inspiration. DJ

Nothing so boldly owns the night
    as owls patrolling treelines.
    Tiny heartbeats, huddle below,
    trembling in the moonshine.
    At dawn, the watch is taken by
    the eagles of the lake,
    Who surveil the landscape far and wide
    for unwary tread or wake.
    The fox slides through dusk's shadows
    treading strips of light
    Hunting for the foragers
    slinking through the night

Most of Oshkosh lives a life
    In varied grades of lumens.
    Under sharp eyes rarely seen,
    They own the world, not humans.

The Kiss

I've always had this odd fascination with Mt. Everest and the people who climb it. I have asthma. It's not a possibility. I even created a board game about it once and made my students play it. DJ

The storm scoured him with shards of ice and his eyes were frozen shut, or were they frozen open? He clung to the side of Mt. Everest like a gnat on an uncaring gray elephant and wondered what his sister Jen was doing. Did she realize he was stuck in the Death Zone, the area above 8000 meters where your body began to eat itself, your brain swelled and your lungs filled with fluids? Her response would be sarcastic and scathing like the winds that held him tight against the ice.

He was going to make it. His energy was still good. His stamina had been compared to the legendary Sherpa climbers who were born on the mountain. Some study said their thicker skin and thinner blood allowed them to thrive in the oxygen depleted air. They were alpine gods and so was he.

Sherpas believed that climbers who died on the mountain must be brought down or their spirits would linger near their bodies forever. Since it was so freaking dangerous to drag a frozen body down the treacherous mountain, most climbers agreed to have their body dropped in any nearby crevasse rather than put rescuers in peril.

Ken laughed when the expedition discussed it and said he and his twin Jen had matching burial plots in Wisconsin. He was coming down the mountain. His body shook so hard, he banged against the ice. Shivering was good. He still had time.

If you didn't summit by two pm on Mt. Everest, you turned around and started planning for next year. Otherwise, climbers risked descending in complete darkness and brutal cold. A summit after 2pm was a death sentence for most. But he wasn't most climbers.

He and another experienced climber, Rolf, left the group and continued up. It was a selfish decision to go on once his team turned back, but climbing was a selfish endeavor as his twin Jen often pointed out. He was fast, though, freaky fast. He would make it.

Rolf stopped after a couple of hours. He couldn't keep up. Like many who died on Everest, he just sat down and gave up. After a few tries to rouse him, Ken continued around him on the narrow trail. It wasn't callous; it was what you did on the big mountain. Trying to save people just got everyone killed.

Ken hadn't counted on the freak storm. At first, the weather was perfect and the winds manageable, but it was a ruse. The storm hit like a hammer and when he tried to crest the Hilary Step; he got blown backwards. It was a miracle and a tribute to his strength that he wasn't blown off the ridge. As the winds approached hurricane strength, he was pinned to the ice just below the summit.

He relaxed against the sheer rock face. At a 70 degree inclination, it was the only thing he could do as the storm whipped around him. The tingling pain in his legs and feet had come and gone hours ago, or was it days?

A few people had survived a night on the big mountain. He shoved his frozen hands deeper into the ice. He would make it. If anyone could, it was him. The storm went on into eternity.

****

At base camp, his twin, Jen checked her gear again. She was bringing not one, not two, but three Sherpas. They would do all the work, but she wanted to go as far as possible with them. They would continue on if she turned back and bring Ken's body down.

She'd begun training when Ken did, and she was in the best shape of her life. "You should join us on the expedition," Ken joked, but Jen saw no point in conquering a rock, as she called it.

When his group came down without him, she knew, in the mysterious way of those who shared a womb, that he was dead. They advised her to wait. People had walked out of a storm before. Miracles could happen.

What did they know? They weren't twins. She was going to get him. The night before they left, she dreamt she was frozen in the ice. She woke drenched in cold sweat with hands and feet numb, determined to find him.

****

She climbed easily, and the Sherpas joked she might join their ranks. Between grief and muscle pain, she struggled with self doubt and wondered if they should go on without her. The Khumba Ice flow cooperated, and she was blessed with perfect weather.

They found him where he'd tried to last out the storm. He was trapped; arms frozen into the ice as if he were part of the mountain. The Sherpas sighed. They would have to chip out his corpse.

The head Sherpa asked respectfully if she wanted to go on to the summit with one of them while they used their pickaxes to free him. By the time she got back, they would have the body packaged and ready to go down. The sound of the chipping ice forced tears out of her eyes, so she motioned for the guide to lead the way.

Technically, once past the Hillary Step, the climbing is simple. Their climb had been blessed by Mt. Everest's standards. She stayed a moment at the summit, admiring the view and wondering if Ken had been on his way up or down when the storm hit.

When she returned to the Sherpas, her brother's corpse was ready, rolled in heavy plastic and trussed like a roast. His head was still exposed, and she leaned over and whispered, "I get it, Ken. I get why you do this." She kissed his forehead, the skin cold and unyielding.

****

He felt the spark of dawn over the peaks as the storm retreated. Warmth touched his forehead like a kiss and his spirit soared into the thin clouds over the top of the world.

The Wave

This story used to have a little green man in it. My husband objected to it, now the little green man from the ocean depths is gone. My husband wants me to put him back in but he exists in no version I can find. DJ

I sipped my all-inclusive Sangria while working on a magazine quiz on my life's achievements: marriage, motherhood, divorce, pretty sparse.

The bartender servicing the beach ran past me, spraying crystal white sand on my magazine. His brown legs were muscled and glistened in the hot sun. I admired the view, but then I saw the problem.

The ocean had receded and little fish struggled in their new, airy environment. Seaweed was enormous. Who knew? As the water pulled back to the sea, a Discovery special on tsunamis flashed before my bifocals. Water pulling away from the beach, check, a long wave building on the horizon, waiting to kill everyone, check.

As I pondered whether to run or finish my drink, my 50-year-old body made its decision. Those dormant flight or fight responses functioned perfectly.

As I tried to call up the tips from Discovery, I remembered to avoid the hotel. I grabbed one of the bikes for rent as I churned my fat legs up the hill, going past the hotel.

A little brown-skinned man at the bike rental place yelled at me. He hadn't seen the coming terror yet. I sent him a silent apology and pedalled with legs that hadn't exercised since the Reagan era.

I hit a rock and became a middle-aged projectile. Landing dazed in the grass, I watched death roll in.

The swelling water chased a paunchy middle-aged man with his lovely young friend from the beach. I almost smiled as I imagined them to be my ex husband and his mistress. The old guy ran well for someone who lived his life behind a desk. The wave swept past them and moved up the hill relentlessly.

Beyond the glistening hotel on the other side of the hill behind me was a land raked by poverty that I hadn't noticed.

Everyone said divorce is a new beginning, and it was. I could barely pay the bills every month. As soon as the papers were signed, my ex littered his Facebook with pictures of a Club Sex vacation. My chest hurt and I spent my savings on this trip.

The only vacation we'd ever taken was in a crowded car with two kids to the Grand Canyon. One of the kids had horrible gas. Never did find out which one. It could have been both. We laughed a lot though and slept in the stifling car at night to save money.

I spared a thought for the people in the hotel whose first inkling of death was water sliding up the stairwells.

The wave slid up my hill and I found running was still an option. It caught up to me and lifted me gently amidst chunks of debris and a few floating bodies.

I wasn't a great swimmer but I Michael Phelp's my way to bushes that ended up being the tops of palm trees. I held on, digging my nails into what wood I could find. If I survived, I would need a serious manicure.

A branch cruised by and I realized it was returning to sea. The wave was receding! A passing branch clipped my arm, and the break resonated through my body. I gratefully passed out.

I woke 30 feet up in a palm tree with the really serious pain you hope to only read about. They would need a crane to rescue me. Waves like that come in series, don't they? Had I missed the next one or two? The Discovery Channel blurred in my mind. The sun rode high in the sky and waves of heat parched my throat. I couldn't yell and could only wave with one arm.

Below, I saw the man whose bike I took. He took off his shirt and looped it behind the tree. I had seen this on TV, but it was fascinating in person. He made his way easily up the tree.

Was he coming up to yell at me about the bike? It seemed petty.

"Hey, sorry about the bike. Could you call a crane or the fire department, please?" Every rib on his thin frame was visible, but when he got to me, he wasn't even breathing hard.

He smiled and his teeth were perfect. He wedged himself against a branch and pulled me off my perch. Can I confide that I outweighed him by a hundred pounds? He positioned me in a weird sort of fireman's carry so he could use both of his hands going down.

I repeated, "Hail Mary Full of Grace," over and over, which was all I knew of the Rosary, being Protestant.

And then we thudded to the ground. The smell hit me: rotting vegetation with a side of corpses baking in the sun.

He squatted and let me scramble off his back. "Thank you," I managed. I vowed to buy him a new bike, maybe a Schwinn. He walked away, but I trudged after him in the steaming sand. He was my only friend here.

What I had done in my life so far had been fine, a good effort as far as it went. I just hadn't had the opportunity to be all I could be.

Opportunity didn't happen to overweight divorcees who watched TV from the couch every night and cried in their Cheetos.

He led me to another islander who tore shreds off his shirt to splint my arm. When he repositioned it, my whole world tilted and my vision tunneled to a focused point. In that new vision, I saw a world of people who needed me. A chance to make a real difference.

I would stay and help the islanders. Maybe work in a school or a hospital, wherever they needed me. Nothing tied me to my old life and it would be a while before I was able to leave, anyway. I could stay and find my place here.

They needed me but right now, but it was a toss-up who needed whom more.

The interview

Ouija boards scare the crap out of me. DJ

"Just get it, Kezia." Anna ordered. My hands shook and I twisted them together to hide it. My chest threatened to squeeze the air from my lungs. I glanced at the door to the basement. I could sprint up the stairs, across the street and be in my bedroom sanctuary with a good book in under a minute. And ruin any chance of having friends in high school, ever.

WWTSD? What would Taylor Swift do? I drew in a deep belly breath and a belch of pepperoni pizza popped out as I struggled to stand. Swear to God my knees did not knock together although Neon snickered. I glanced around at the three girls assessing me and made my choice. I knew where the Ouija board was because I buried it a few minutes ago under a pile of games after we did our nails on it. Mine were "Screaming Teal" and they matched Anna's. I didn't want to touch the stupid board when we *weren't* using it to summon something foul. Now it froze the blood in my veins.

I could do scary movies if the bad guys were, like, human or aliens that looked like humans. Giant, evil insects bent on Earth's destruction were disgusting but I could handle them. The supernatural stuff, not so much. My heritage was what screwed me up. I'm Gypsy on my dad's side. When he died two years ago, my mom took us away from the clan and plunked us into middle class suburbia. The gypsies were all, like, symbols and omens. They don't move a step without consulting some dead bug or something. Even though I knew it was all stupid, I still get those bad vibes, the heebie jeebies, around spooky stuff. My teeth clench and a hot steel ball races around my stomach until bile crawls up my throat and makes me want to yak.

In fact, I had puked during a late night babysitting gig this summer. I fell asleep on the Hagan's couch and when I snapped to, some black and white movie with Devil worship was in full black mass. Sour sweat sprang out of my pores, my stomach did an inward half gainer and I was up and running for the toilet. I harked up popcorn and Dr. Pepper with only a disgusted cat as my witness. Appropriate, since cats are the protectors of Gypsies.

Tonight was a turning point, an interview of sorts. These girls were seeing if they liked me enough to be friends. Being invited on a sleepover gave me five Awesome Points and I sure didn't want to lose them over some idiotic thing that could only last, how long? Twenty minutes? I could do this if I really had to.

I was jacked Anna asked me: third week of high school, no less. I wasn't someone she hung with. OK, Truth: I didn't hang with anyone. Last week, everyone in bio laughed at the same time when their Snapchat went off except me and Diana, the Goth chick. She scrutinized her flat black hair for split ends but I decided right then I needed a plan. I needed a BFF: A Best Friend Forever seemed within my abilities and cheaper than a cell phone. I came up with the Awesome Point system. It's like Weight Watchers without the food.

I kept track of my points in a tiny notebook hidden in my pillowcase and I tried to be fair. The system seemed to be reaping me big benefits when I got invited to this sleepover.

I grabbed the board and was blinded! My sight was gone; everything went black. A shrill scream like tearing glass started and the lights snapped back on.

"Was that you, Kezia? I just turned off the lights," Anna was backed against the wall, hanging on the light switch like it was holding her up. Neon was in a defensive crouch, ready to fight and Marcy sat in the leather recliner glaring at me with enormous owl-eyes.

"Sorry," I mumbled, throwing the board to the carpet in front of Neon. She locked eyes with me as she lit a red candle with holly around it, some Christmas leftover with too much wax to toss. The heavy red drops joined and then pooled around the yellow wick.

"Lights are going off," Anna called out to no one in particular.

Neon's white blond hair reflected the light of the candle. It was buzzed on the sides so her scalp showed and one big thick lock hung over her face. Why couldn't I be more like her? She was fearless; a tiger in a tiny package.

She wore skirts so short you could almost see her butt cheeks and ripped black nylons. Hayden, the biggest jock in the school put his hand up her skirt in the lunchroom and she launched off her tiny feet and knocked him out with a right cross that would have made an MMA fighter smile. She didn't get in trouble for it either or not as much as you'd think. And you knew, just knew, she'd do it again if someone hassled her. I didn't envy her the Don't-Give-A-Rat's-Ass what you do parents, but maybe that was part of her gig.

Marcy completed our foursome. Marcy, plain as white yogurt but seriously smart. She could have been pretty but chose not to, IMHO. I mean, she had thick brown hair down her back and this heart shaped face with large blue eyes. A few highlights, some contacts and she would be gorgeous. She told us she was happier viewing the world through inch thick glasses that always had smudges on them.

My wavy hair is almost black, almost curly and not even close to tameable. It was really long until we left the clan and my mom had it cut. Now, it's stupid and makes like a halo around my head and I'm growing it out again, painful day by painful day. My eyes are really dark and my lashes are pretty good. Better if I was allowed to use mascara. I'm thin and my skin is dusky according to my mom and Mexican if you listen to jerks in the lunchroom, which I get tired of hearing. Same-O, Lame-O. My skin is pretty clear though and for that, I'm grateful. Zits on top of everything? Gag me.

I sat facing Neon, with Marcy on my right and Anna on my left. Please God, don't make us hold hands. Mine are wet and clammy. If I survive this, I'll do something good, I promise, like visit the old folk's home once a week, maybe. I like old people except for the smell; they're quiet inside somehow. Gypsies never send their Elders away from the family. I miss the Mamsa Jenkins, she smelled like jasmine and told fortunes. She always had time for me.

"Put your hands on the plastic thing," Anna whispered. I saw everyone else's painted nails already there and added my "Screaming Teal" to the mix.

"Is there a spirit out there? Come talk to us." Neon intoned.

I was swallowing like crazy but all the spit had left my mouth.

"Maybe we don't want anything to come," I whispered.

"It's the energy in our hands. Nothing is going to happen," Marcy's eyes rolled.

"If there is a spirit, make yourself known," Neon said.

I swear that plastic pointer thing moved. I didn't do it and Neon's mouth dropped open. Marcy's lips thinned into a line and Anna gasped.

N-O the pointer read.

"Ask it why not?" said Anna.

"Why won't you come, spirit?" Neon said.

The pointer moved quickly spelling H-E-R and stopped.

"Her. What does that mean?" Anna demanded.

"Sounds like it wants someone else to invite it," offered Marcy.

"I'll ask it," Anna said. "Is it me, spirit?"

The pointer didn't budge.

"Is it me, spirit?" Marcy spoke but no go. Shit.

"Kezia, ask it," whispered Neon.

Breathless, I mumbled, "Me?"

Y-E-S

Nervous giggles from the girls, blood in my mouth.

"Ask it why you?" said Anna, affronted.

The pointer slid. W-I-T-C-H.

"Cool, you're a witch," said Neon.

How does one react to this news with awesomeness? I was hard put to manage.

"Ask it if you have any powers," Neon said.

I didn't want any powers. I didn't want any more bile shooting up the back of my throat either but tonight was out of my hands.

"Do I have any powers?" I ventured. I'd seen the Avengers. Powers might be fun. I could hang with Loki who was rumored to be nice as well as sexy in his alter ego of Tom Hiddleston.

The light in the room rose like on a dimmer switch and holy shit, the hottest guy I've ever seen was standing just outside our circle. Looking at me. I clutched hands with the girls on either side of me. Just instinct, I guess and the smoldering man frowned. Motes of glitter floated around him, swirling as he moved.

"No need to fear me. I mean you no harm," his voice was like hot chocolate, smooth and tempting. "You invited me. Let's go somewhere we can talk, privately, like Paris." He smiled and held out a well shaped hand to me.

"No, I'm not leaving my friends." My heart pounded against my ribs like it was going to fly out.

"They aren't your friends, Kezia, not really. I can show you things, marvelous things. Give you access to powers, *chovani*." The Romani word for witch rolled out of his beautiful mouth and shivers marched up my back. "Help your mom so she doesn't have to work two jobs."

Images swirled around the room, glittering, shimmering. Me as I wanted to be: tall, slim, with boobs and a long dark cloud of hair. My mom relaxing and smiling at me. Famous people begging to be my friends. Somewhere, Anna's cat screamed and it all faded.

"No thanks," I said with a lot more confidence than I felt. Anna squeezed my hand. "What's the catch? What's the *bibaxt*?" I asked. It meant "bad luck" or "price" in Romanji.

He smirked and didn't look quite as cute as before. "You become one with me, after all is said and done and you've lived a full, glorious life."

"Exactly how does that happen?" The thing with demons, or so Mamsa Jenkins told me, was they couldn't lie if you asked them a direct question. The trick was, knowing the questions to ask.

He avoided my eyes. When he finally raised his head, I saw his bright blue eyes were glowing orange. "I eat your soul and any remaining body parts."

"Fuck," whispered Anna. All three pairs of eyes snapped to her. Anna never swore.

"Language!" Mocked Neon and we all giggled. Air came to me again and I noticed his hand was more of a claw. Anna's cat bumped into my back, hard. It broke my fascination with the slender, almost perfect being.

"Many have believed the journey worthy of the destination," he said. The cat swept across my back and then turned and nudged me with her other side. The only place I was warm was where the cat touched me. I began to focus on that warmth, like a lifeline.

"I'll keep these friends and my life," I told him and felt the cat purr against my back.

"We revoke our stupid invitation. Leave Kezia alone," Neon shouted.

"Yeah, she's our friend," Marcy added.

"And get out of my house, loser." Anna jumped up breaking our circle and hitting the lights. I blinked once and wiped a hand across my damp eyes. I didn't care if they thought I was lame. I was way beyond caring. Neon put a bony arm across my shoulder and Anna handed me a tissue. The cat crawled into my lap and ran a rough tongue across my hand.

"Whoa. Look at that," Marcy pointed towards the basement door. Footprints on the carpet, deep impressions only just beginning to spring back as if from a great weight.

The Natural Leader

Part of my Voo Doo era. I may still be in it. DJ

The rain fell slow and hot in the town of Harvest on the day we put Mamman Melinda into the ground. And looking at the hopeless faces of the townspeople, I realized no one expected her to stay there long.

The day before, I had cut off her hands with reluctance and driven them to the ocean in a plastic container filled with bricks and wrapped liberally in duct tape. The requisit chicken squawked in a crate in the backseat. Chickens are always available here in the back country and no one, I repeat no one, wants to know whether you're making soup or a zombie. Your chicken- your business.

When I got to the bright ocean, I spent hard-earned money to hire a boat with sonar and I drove it around until I found a reasonably deep spot. There, I sang a few words in the tongue of my people and killed the chicken, splashing blood liberally over the plastic and duct tape. I'd better be sprucing up my rituals, I thought with a frown. People love a good ritual. I added a Christian prayer for icing and heaved the container and chicken remains over the side. What can I say? I'm a mom so I did the best I could.

I popped open a can of soda, blowing out a sigh of relief. What's done is done. My strategy seemed infallible under yesterday's pale aqua sky. The hands would be hard for Melinda to retrieve without a lot of difficulty. She would have a tough time casting spells without them.

But, today with the rain steaming off the fresh earth of her grave like an accusing ghost, I was wondering what the hell I had done. And what the hell I was going to do now.

Since I had killed the high priestess, I had the crown for now. Could I really fill the vacancy? I believed in the Vodun down to my soul. Vodun or Voodoo as some called it, was a delicate balance of missionary Christianity and belief in spirits of the earth. I made sure my son was exposed to both so he could make his own path when he got older. My husband, Bill, God rest his soul, had allowed this.

With the stakes as high as they were, maybe just maybe I could be the High Priestess until I figured a wayy out of this mess. If the people lost confidence in me, some man or woman might feel they could do a better job. Replacing me might or might not involve bloodshed. I had to protect my son as long as I could.

So, this morning when the funeral director offered me the rubber apron and the electric saw, I was a bit shaky but I took them just the same. He discretely left the room and I had to figure out the safety and the on switch, but I managed ok.

When chunks of flesh whipped up on my chin, I kept my eyes on the prize and finished what I had to do.

We keep a thin veneer of civilization here in Harvest. Everyone knew if Melinda didn't have her hands when she rose, devastation would only be delayed until she could find them. Unless a new leader was so strong Melinda couldn't rise. At the funeral, you could see the shadow of disaster in the people's eyes. Melinda would likely wreck havoc on everyone for what I'd done.

At the source of this whole mess is my son, Josh. To me, he is just my son, but to others, he is one gorgeous hunk of man. I have this on good authority. The hairdresser tells me so. The grocery clerk mentions it every week when I check out. The bus driver ogles him and even the gay traffic cop has confirmed his perfection. Teenage girls giggle it over the phone breathlessly before hanging up. And don't think I don't recognize your laugh, Charisse! Grown women sigh when he walks by them.

When he is doing yard work with his shirt off, there is a gallery of onlookers. He is a solid six feet two inches of muscle over a lean frame. His shoulders are broad and his waist is impossibly slim. He had soulful dark eyes and a head of unruly curly hair.

He wants to be a paramedic after high school so he can help the people of Harvest. Josh is a natural born leader. Women adore him but guys like him too.

My husband was a colonel in the rangers doing something only rangers do, when he passed. He wasn't an Adonis, like Josh. He had an ugly mass of burn scars across his chest and face that gave him a sinister look, most shied away from. Nobody messed with him in Harvest. Not that he was around much. I hadn't seen him for months when the man with all the medals on his uniform came to my door to tell me he was dead.

That was when the trouble began. High Priestess or not, Melinda didn't muck with my Bill. He was scary on a whole 'nother level. He wouldn't have stopped with cutting off her hands, I thought. Nothing would have been found of her and no one would ever have known.

She wasn't as afraid of me, but maybe she should have been.

When I went to the Vodun circle the night after I heard that my Bill wasn't coming home, I expected some comfort from the people of Harvest on the death of my man. Josh stayed home, in his own world of sorrow.

Mamman Melinda informed me with no preamble that she was taking my Josh for her mate. That he was 18 and had his own plans had no impact on her. She was 55 years old if she was a day and the affront of her claiming my son when I had just learned of my husband's death was too much.

I stood there with my eyes stinging as she pulled out her ceremonial knife and made a small cut on my arm. She would use the blood, she told me, to bind Josh to her.

I could not let her take my blood. Beside binding Josh, she could easily use it to killl me or drive me insane. And then who would protect my son? I grabbed her skinny, jiggly arm with the knife in it, intent on retrieving my blood when she yanked on the knife and it thwacked into her chest with a wet sound.

She stared at me, wild eyed as she slid to the ground. The circle of onlookeers looked at her body. Their eyes lifted to me, waiting for me to do something.

Mersus Wade, the funeral director, came forward and asked if I would like him to take care of the body. Just a formality. I nodded dumbly and he whispered I should come by early the next morning. Things were happening too fast and I had a horrible feeling there was a bad ending hurtling towards me that I couldn't even see yet.

Josh was scarce this morning, so I was able to complete the boat adventure and get cleaned up at home before going to the High Priestess ceremony. I headed out into the warm, clear night. The rain washed away the stench of industry from the island and maybe it could make me clean too. My strides grew more confident. The fire was already burning and the circle was full of the people of Harvest. I would try to move the community back to where we needed to be: good people working together to get through this life.

I went to the platform that served as the position of honor. I gazed at the faces surrounding me and felt a strange unease. Would my son be an orphan before the night was through? I knew if I died, the people of Harvest would make sure he was alright.

Josh stepped from outside the circle into the firelight. Would he be forced to witness my death? Despite the warm night, icy fingers clenched my heart. I loved him so much and he was all I had left. The firelight played off his face and I noticed he was naked except for a small skirt the men wore for ceremonies. Like air filling a sail, a sigh went through the circle. He smiled broadly at me.

"Hey, mom!" His voice boomed out into the circle. "What are you doing up there? You don't want to lead Harvest." His voice carried into the watchful night. He knew nothing of fear. He grinned and something in my heart broke with love for him.

"No, I don't but I will. I owe them this and will do my best." We spoke as if it was just the two of us in my kitchen.

"Get down from there. These good people deserve a leader who wants to lead. One who is strong enough to balance today with yesterday and tomorrow."

"But who will care for these People? They need someone to bless children and marriages, comfort the elder and be their spritual guide." I began to panic thinkiing of all the things a good leader provided for their people. We had been without them for so long.

"Oh, Mom!" Josh laughed and jumped up on the platform. As I looked around the circle, I realized not only was he theirs but they were his.

Last Dance

From when my hip first started giving it up. DJ

"Your hip is disintegrating. It's really fascinating, from a medical perspective. You don't usually see someone so young with such advanced deterioration. We can't even do a hip replacement. It's amazing you can walk at all." The doctor smiled at me, almost giddy. He was very handsome, in that way Latin males have, dark and creamy like good ale.

He could probably dance all night and operate all day. He looked barely out of his teens. Was he some kind of wunderkind who graduated from med school at twelve? His nametag wasn't large enough to contain all the letters of his name. I hadn't gotten to choose my guy. He was the only choice in the HMO. His speech had the lilt of someone born on the other side of the world.

On the plus side, he had the best looking eyebrows I'd ever seen on a man. Smooth olive skin and a nose that might have been lovingly crafted by a surgeon's knife.

"It's interesting to me from the perspective that I can barely walk and I'm in excruciating pain all the time." I lay in the hospital bed, smothered by a blanket that stank of the same disinfectant that permeates all evil places. Would the smell cling to me? My skin began to itch and a small spasm raced from my left buttock to my ribs. I gasped and my eyes watered as I fought to move air through my reluctant lungs.

"We could put a big pin into the hip to lock it up but it won't stop the degeneration. The pain is the tough thing to manage." He smiled again.

"Manage as in it is never going to abate?" The former English teacher in me loved the feel of words and used them freely.

"Abate?" He raised one perfect eyebrow.

"Like mosquito abatement. Make the pain stop. Will the rod in my hip make me walk upright again?" I walked with an unattractive, hunched over gait, leaning to one side like a ship sinking. It made breathing hard as my lungs were compressed.

"No, we can't stop you from folding over because you've already got some serious damage. We can manage the pain but not eliminate it. It's going to get to the point where we run out of things that will help." Now, he put on his serious face.

The pain was my seat belt. Everything I wanted to do from laundry to dancing the fandango, required my hip. Only, most of the hip wasn't there anymore so the muscles did the best they could and spasmed when they couldn't cover the spread.

He left with a swirl of his lab coat and a hearty handshake. Don't let the door hit you, I thought. I almost said it out loud, but if this guy was going to be my main drug dealer, I didn't want him getting stingy.

The nurse came back and handed me the new, scary prescription.

"What do you think?" In my opinion, nurses know the skinny on just about everything. When my mom was due to get released from the hospital, the nurse told us to stay even though the doctor had signed the release. Mom died of a stroke that day. Nurses know shit.

"You're screwed. A rod in your ass isn't going to get you dancing shoes sweetie."

Thank you, Jesus, for drive-through prescription pick up. When the pain started ramping up, I found grocery stores that delivered and laundry services that picked up. I shook the small bottle of pills. They rationed how many you could get at one time. The colorful warning labels did nothing at all to make it festive. If I took them all at once, would it end this?

The pharmacist had warned me against even taking two, despite crippling pain. I made myself a perfect cup of coffee. Added a little cream, expired, but only just, and that seemed to fit. I wound it into my coffee like a silk scarf. I would miss coffee.

I poured the pills into my shaking hand. Like small jewels, they glittered, each with a golden drop of poison in the gel casing. I slung the lot of them into the back of my throat. I chased them down with coffee and smiled.

I was tired, so tired. He swam into my vision and I tried hard to focus on him. It was worth it. He looked a lot like my doctor, but sexy and dangerous. He was the kind of man you read about in romance novels who made women scream in ecstasy. Instead of his white lab coat, he wore a tuxedo and snow white shirt. I never understood the tuxedo fascination till just that moment. I realized I would have eaten him, he looked so good. I inhaled and caught the elusive scent of him, like burnt caramel over vanilla.

He spun and then did a graceful sketch step. He held out his hand, a long, beautifully formed hand, towards me. I had only to put my hand in his and be done with this life. All the pain and suffering gone. All the embarrassment of seeing the wreckage I had become. I understood what it meant to put my hand in his. I would dance the last dance with a grace that Ginger Rodgers never knew.

But wait. There was a heavy price tag attached and I knew it. I would be taking the chicken shit route out of the game. Was I that desperate to cha cha one more time like my hair was on fire?

I wasn't halfway through my bucket list. What about climbing Mt. Everest? I didn't want to, but when the possibility was taken from me, it hurt. When did I get to fall in love and marry? Was there a Mr. Igor out there for me? There was still some fight in me. If you can't be a fine example, be bad enough to be a warning. I could certainly be a bad example. I could take up smoking cigars and playing poker all night.

The guy in the tux looked annoyed. I noticed he had an overbite with sharp little fangs peeking out. He wasn't as hot anymore. In fact, he reminded me of a particularly unpleasant student I'd had. And the smell had more burnt than sweet to it. He tapped a big cloven hoof, waiting. For what? For me to finish killing myself? Crap on that.

I dialed 911 on my phone and told them I'd had a change of heart. Then, I crawled to the bathroom and stuck my finger down my throat like I'd seen the thin girls do in the bathroom. I was a newbie at it, but I think I did myself proud. Tiny jewels sparkled in the viscous puke and I thought they were too late, perhaps. I counted my heartbeats as I drifted away.

When I opened my eyes, a gorgeous young man had his lips clamped tightly against mine. He had a heavy yellow coat on. He leaned back and smiled at me. I smiled back at him and asked, "May I have this dance?"

The Moon Trees

Aboard the Apollo 14 mission in 1971, was Stuart Roosa, former US Forest Service smoke jumper. As part of a public relations initiative, he brought hundreds of tree seeds to be germinated and dispersed throughout the United States as part of the nation's bicentennial in 1976. Although they never touched the surface of the moon, they orbited it. They were called the Moon Trees. The list of where the seedlings were planted is incomplete with only a quarter of the trees accounted for.

from NASA.gov

1970

Packets of seeds slid across Martin's polished work space.

"These are going on Apollo 14?" All the freight that went to the moon came through the Center to be weighed, logged and labeled before it went on board.

"Yes, we'll ship them with the package." The project manager wore a crisp white lab coat although Martin had never seen him do any actual work that might generate the need to protect his business suit.

"Seeds?"

"It's a public relations stunt. We send them up to see if cosmic radiation does anything but we already know it's not going to. Then, we give the trees away all over the country and everyone will feel like they're a part of NASA."

"So, the seeds soak up space radiation, store it in their cells and when they grow something happens?"

"Ridiculous, I know but the "Moon Trees" will make good copy and every city will want one." He shrugged.

"Loblolly pine, sycamore, sweetgum, redwood and Douglas fir," Martin said reading the label. "These are all southern and western species. Where are the maples and oaks?" Martin came from Wisconsin where sturdy oaks reached for the sky.

"No idea." His supervisor walked away.

Martin locked the packets of seeds away and took his lunch outside. He sat in the picnic area under the shade of a generous oak. Even in January, it was warm and humid in Florida. His lunch bag blew off the table and he bent to pick it up. Almost as an afterthought, he scooped up a handful of acorns, their little caps fitted snugly like helmets. Martin slid them into his lab coat pocket.

Present

"This is the last time I'm giving samples," Rusty was proud that his voice remained firm.

The doctors turned in sync to look at his mom. He warned her not to say a thing. She turned away crying, always crying. No help there.

"Rusty, you're helping save the lives of other children. I realize there is discomfort, but your sacrifice..." the doctor droned on.

"Sacrifice is right. You're skinning me alive. I can't even take pain meds because it might screw up your stupid experiments. I'm so done with this." He slid off the cold metal table, pushing through the sea of white lab coats that fluttered like moth wings. He heard his mother sniffling in his wake, felt the unspoken apology in her eyes.

She was dead to him and he didn't care if she knew it. She already signed his body away when he died. Who signed away a nine year old? She didn't think he knew it, but he saw the papers when she fell asleep one night. When he passed, she would hit a number on her speed dial and a special team would helicopter in and take him. It sounded really cool and he was sorry he would miss it. Life was a bitch when you're nine and people were waiting for you to die. All because she'd birthed a genetic retard. He was the only person with whatever it was he had. In the whole frickin' world. Sorry for the inconvenience but I've still got some time on the clock. Not a lot, but some. He turned in the car and yelled at his mother.

"And I"m going on the scout trip this weekend."

"Honey, the chance for infection is too high."

"I'm going or I'll run away and you'll never get your pound of flesh," he threatened, pleased to see his mother shake with fear.

Rusty was having a blast. He was just a regular kid here at camp. Mr. Hooper maybe asked him too many times if he was feeling tired, but that was a minor annoyance. He ran over a log bridge when his leg gave way. He covered it so the other kids thought he was clumsy. One kid even offered him an inhaler like he had asthma or something. He should be so lucky.

The disease was coming for him sooner rather than later. Maybe even this weekend. He wouldn't mind dying out here among the trees. He wanted to stay away from hospitals and doctors with their bright scalpels. He could take the pain, for the most part. They were old friends. It was the needles or the way the doctors were so eager to scrape away at him, killing him layer by layer.

Unlike most of the campers, Rusty was grateful when the counselors made them take a nap in the afternoon. There was supposed to be a freakin' cool meteor shower tonight. A once in a lifetime display of astral fireworks and he was determined to see it.

"Just get me through tonight," he asked as he lay on his sleeping bag. Confident that the universe heard his plea, he let the pain wash over and through him while he waited for the cool night to come.

Footsteps echoed on the wooden floor, and Rusty's eyes snapped open. Mr. Hooper's silhouette in the door of the cabin with a glowing red flashlight. Rusty made sure his flashlight had the protective cover of cellophane on it before he switched it on, so he wouldn't screw up his night vision. He ran out into the cool night and looked up. Billions of stars welcomed him to the event.

He followed the line of red lights that reminded him of red corpuscles flowing through veins until he reached the clearing. Trees reached up their bare limbs to cradle the stars, and all for me, Rusty thought. Thank you.

There were too many meteors to count and Rusty struggled to retch quietly as dizziness and nausea hit him. The whole sky was moving and he fought the feeling of vertigo.

When he turned back to the clearing, kids began screaming and running in all directions, followed by panicked camp counselors. A large fireball crawled across the sky towards him. He felt feverish and imagined its heat. This one's for me, he smiled. The cool night held him like a cocoon, and he was alone in the clearing.

The ground rumbled and shook and Rusty fell. The sound followed, a terrifying bellow as the meteor exploded above him. Rock ash and shards of ice rained down on him but he kept looking up and smiling. This was the end, he could feel it. Liquid bled from his ears as his eardrums burst and his grin continued.

As he looked across the clearing into the woods, he saw one tree illuminated. Its smooth bark shiny gray in the silver glow of the starlight. He walked towards it on aching joints as the disease fed on him. The tips of the branches pulsed with light like a firefly at dusk. He broke off a low-lying tip but the dazzling fire in it remained. His fingers tingled where the sap ran onto them. He stuck his finger in his mouth.

An explosion of sugar, no something better than sugar, more like energy filled his mouth. He ate one after another until all the low-lying ones were naked. His vision blurred and he sat at the base of the tree. It smoldered and the heat rose in ghostly tendrils.

The searing heat began in his mouth. He screamed and writhed as it traveled through his insides, ripping away the disease from his DNA. His last vision was of the stars dancing overhead.

He woke and the tree was just a tree again. The stars moved slowly in the heavens and nothing fell from the skies. Whatever energy the tree had possessed, was gone. Only a silvery oak remained. Where before the pain had defined his existence, now there was only a hollow echo of where the pain had been. He felt good. He felt better than good, he felt well. He hugged the tree and ran back to camp.

The Timebomb

From my years of teaching highschool. DJ

"Well, yes, thank you for asking, my life sucks," Jes made a face in the mirror. She daubed the heavy coverage makeup on her cheek with a square of rough toilet paper. The creamy make up pot was two thirds empty. When times were tough, the weak use cover up. She was an idiot, what could she say? She moved to get a better look at her face under the dim bulb in the trailer bathroom. She couldn't do much about the swelling except ice and she was bordering on late to school already.

She grabbed some ice out of the freezer and held it on her cheek briefly and then her wrist.

"Okay, that's unpleasant," she winced. The bruising was just starting on her pale skin. She dragged down her sleeve so the ripped part didn't show and her bruised wrist was covered. Haute couture was the same hoodie she wore every lame day of her passion play.

Her mom lay on the couch where she'd passed out after their brief fight this morning. Jes tucked a threadbare afghan around her. Her mom always started pounding whiskey when dad tangled with the cops.

She grabbed her large cloth bag and considered the gun laying on the counter. Should she take it or leave it? Would her mom wake up before she got back from school was the question?

Two giant, unsmiling policemen had jammed into their tiny trailer at four in the morning, the witching hour for drunks to get home after last call. Jes was sleeping on the fold out bench when the lights snapped on. They had her dad cuffed and gone before she even fully woke up. Her mom pulled out the whiskey then and found the gun in the cabinet shortly after. Jes hated these kind of mean mornings. Everyone was in a pissy mood and she always seemed to take the brunt of it.

Jes wrestled the gun away from her mom but not before her mom smacked her solid across the face and twisted her wrist. She slid the gun into her purse. The weight was comforting plus reaffirmed that her mom wouldn't be able to get to it when she awoke, hungover and feeling like old newspapers.

Jes stepped out into the early bitter fall of southeastern Wisconsin. The wind cut through the soybean fields, brown leaves tearing by her. Jes might as well have been wearing a t-shirt for all the good the hoodie did as a windbreak. She'd made it through last winter without a coat. She would make it this winter too.

She gritted her teeth and quickened her step, hoping the cold would ease the swelling on her cheek. Jes ducked her head as she entered the high school and went directly to the bathroom to see how bad her face looked under full fluorescents.

In the mirror, Jes smoothed the edges of the makeup on her cheek to blend it better and scrunched her hoodie tight against her face. She pulled some of the fiery red hair from the hoodie and covered most of her face. It would have to do. Tomorrow would be tougher as it ripened to purple but it was Saturday and she wouldn't have to go out.

Some girl was sobbing in an open stall, crammed in with two friends. Jes glanced over and felt her cheek throb. It was Galen's girlfriend, all blond and boobs and never wear an outfit twice, Suzaan. What did she have to worry about? Chip a nail, bitch? Jes hated Galen and anyone who swam in his orbit.

Jes left the bathroom and kept her head down in the noisy, smelly hallway. She jumped the first time a locker slammed. When she slid into her physics class, she said a prayer that today was just decorating for homecoming. She wasn't up for much more. WIth the cops coming she hadn't gotten much sleep.

Her stomach rumbled and she was lightheaded as she gripped the back of her chair to steady herself. She was so hungry she felt hollow and the smells of food made her vaguely nauseous

It happened when she'd gone too long without eating. Her mom didn't get paid till tomorrow so

she would just suck it up.

Their physics teacher stood in front of the class fanning a sheaf of papers. "Clear your desks for a pop quiz. Once you are done, you can go decorate because that is clearly more important than your education." He slapped a sheet face down on the desk in front of her and began working his way around the room. "You can work with a partner. Maybe a partner will be able to teach you something about vectors since I apparently haven't been able to." Vectors were easy, what a dickhead.

Galen grabbed up a sheet and locked eyes with her. He was heading her way, dammit. Her gut churned.

She hated him from somewhere deep in her body. He called her "perky" and pretended everyone didn't know he meant her boobs. Of course then, everyone looked at her chest and her face turned that attractive bright red she enjoyed so much. God, she hated him. She wore the oversized, shapeless hoodie everyday just to hide herself. It made her feel only slightly less naked when his eyes raked down her body.

When she thought about his smug smile, her vision narrowed down to a gray tunnel of fierce fire. Who the hell did Galen think he was anyway? Jes shook her hair across her face again. He knew who he was. Entitled, star football quarterback, cheating his way through school. He would get a fat scholarship, marry a tight, hard blond with good dental work and produce two huge aggressive boys who would date rape with impunity.

She slung the purse under her desk and thought hard about the gun. If that jerk only knew the power she had right now.

She wasn't going to shoot Galen, but she imagined seeing his handsome smug face if she pulled the gun on him. She'd love to see his face when her mask dropped and he saw the ferocity of her hate.

"Lame," Galen muttered, "Total douche maneuver to give us a quiz today, but you'll get me through it, won't you, Perky." he said, too quiet for the physics teacher to hear.

Her face burned. She glanced at Nate, sitting facing her. He watched her from under a bunch of runaway curls. Nate had the best hair ever, girl hair, although no one would ever say so to his rough face.

Jes knew he hated the big bouncy curls. Every once in a while, he'd get a buzz cut, which made his dark blue eyes seem huge in his face. Jes wondered what Nate would do if Galen tagged him with a stupid name like Curly. Probably punch him out or say something so threatening, in that deep casual voice of his, that would make everyone step back.

"Wake up, we've got a quiz to ace," Galen pulled out the chair next to her without asking or even looking at her. He was playing for an audience, as he always did. Jes could see his eyes searching for Suzaan, his girlfriend. She was huddled under a mass of blond hair with two other girls. Was she still crying?

"I don't feel like doing a quiz today," Jes spoke softly, turning the paper over. Galen looked at her, his fine gray eyes assessing. His cheekbones were sharp and the shadow of a beard made him look more like a model than a star football player being recruited by big ten colleges.

He opened his mouth to say something, looked at her face, and scanned the room for someone else to work with. "I don't feel like doing anything." She said out loud. "None of it matters."

No one was even listening to her anyway. She could say anything. She was invisible.

Nate frowned across the space of the two desks. "What's going on?"

"What indeed, Jes?" Raush, the physics teacher, came to her desk and towered over her.

She could say anything.

"What does it matter if I know what a vector is? I'm going to end up cleaning motel rooms, like my mom. Or in jail like my dad." She pushed her pencil between her fingers. Her shoulder ached where her mom had yanked her wrist. Her whole arm was on fire.

"Do you really think so?" Raush sat down in her partner seat. Jes couldn't ever remember him taking a seat during class, Ever. For once, the patronizing tone left his voice. He was almost whispering, just loud enough for her to hear, and maybe Nate and Galen. Loser. Jes was floating above them all, nothing touched her. She was fearless. A decision had been made somewhere inside her. A release of pain came so hard and sudden that Jes felt tears on her cheeks.

"Yeah, I do. I won't need vectors where I'm going," she tightened her lips, aware these might be the last words anyone remembered of her. What a legacy, "I won't need vectors where I'm going." Maybe they would put it on her tombstone. The gun in her purse seemed comforting rather than threatening.

"You could be a stripper for a couple of years," Galen leaned into their conversation from across the aisle. He stood up and ground his hips for guffawing laughter.

Jes sighed. Getting mad at Galen was almost too much effort this morning. He was probably right and that made her decision all the more reasonable.

"There are scholarships," Nate's eyes were wide. "You're really smart, Jes."

"You could go to community college and either work towards a degree or transfer the credits. A lot of people do it, Jes," Raush looked over his glasses at her. He had light brown eyes fringed with sparse lashes. Was he married? She didn't even know. There wasn't a ring on his finger but maybe that wasn't allowed during physics, like sandals.

"I'm tired," Jes confessed. "My mom's a wreck. She works so much and the rest of the time, she cries or drinks. We've got a shit load of bills we can't pay. " She wiped her eyes, "Sorry, I didn't get any sleep last night. My dad got picked up again last night. He's back in jail."

"What did he do?" Nate asked.

"Who the hell knows? Whatever it was, he's a three time loser. I probably won't ever see him again." A memory of him holding her when she was younger came to her and she stared at the desk, watching tears fall onto the black surface. She wiped her face with the sleeve of her hoodie and pushed the sleeves up.

Nate started and his eyes burned into hers. He began to stand. Jes yanked down the sleeves and put her hands under the desk. Nate's eyes had gone flat and angry.

"Homecoming is probably making it all worse. I hate these popularity contests. I was never part of the in crowd." Raush muttered. Jes could barely hear him."You can take the quiz another day," Raush said. Only there wasn't going to be another day, she decided. This was the absolute last frickin day she could endure her crappy life.

"I got through school working full time and taking one class at a time in the evenings. It was a lot of work but look at me now, I'm a physicist, teaching morons who can't even draw a vector. I gave up, should have gotten my masters, I still could if I would just get it done. We are each in charge of our own lives' success or failure." Raush chuckled. "Fuck. Listen to me, all positive and everything. Don't listen to me, Jes. I didn't make it, but that doesn't mean you can't." Raush shook his head and got up, jarring the desk in his haste.

Jes stared at her desk. She could feel Nate's eyes on her. Why wouldn't everyone leave her alone?

Jes flipped the quiz over and did both of the problems. They were absurdly easy. Anyone who even half listened in class could figure them out.

Suzaan, pronounced "su Zahn" was heaving with sobs at the next table. A blond clone was comforting her and shooting glares at Galen. Jes frowned. Some shitty drama going on, probably homecoming related. Nothing compared to her life.

She gave her quiz to Mr. Raush and he smiled at her. Nate appeared and held the door open for her. She looked back where she'd been sitting. The purse sat under her desk and she hurried over to get it before she left the classroom. Idiot.

Nate followed her out into the crowded hallway where students decorated for the hall contest. The music in the hall was loud but all Jes could hear was the heavy beat pounding in her chest. Tears filled her eyes and Nate put a hand on her elbow. "Hey, what's going on?"

"Just personal crap," she told him but he didn't release her elbow.

"You know you can talk to me, don't you?"

His eyes were dark blue and he looked out at her from a heavy fringe of wild curls.

"Are you going to the dance tomorrow?" He asked.

"Do I look lame?"

"Well no, Ah, yeah, just wondering." Nate muttered, keeping pace with her down the hall. "So you aren't going to the game either then, huh?"

"Also lame," Jes could only think about how much worse her face would look tomorrow. Besides, today was the End of Days. If anyone could understand, it was Nate and she wanted to tell him but she couldn't.

"So you've got other plans?" Nate said.

"No. I'll be at home." Why was he harassing her? She needed a minute to get her thoughts together.

"Yeah, that sounds way more interesting. Of course, if we did go to the game, we could mock people and have pizza at the game or the dance."

He grinned at her. "Unless you're planning a mass shooting, you could always do it Monday, like if the dance was crappy or we lose the football game." Nate flushed and lowered his eyes to his shoes. She jerked as if he'd hit her. The gun in her purse banged into her thigh.

Nate's head was down as he walked through the crowds in the hallway. "Yeah that was stupid. Who cares about the football game?"

Jes stopped and looked at his face. A single drop of sweat rolled from his temple down his smooth and perfect cheekbone. Jes could see he'd never shaved. She watched the sweat disappear as it travelled. What was going on? She just wanted a few minutes to herself.

She fled ahead of him, out of the crowded hallway into the deserted commons area. Her breath caught in her chest.

"So we don't actually have to decorate, do we?" Nate asked. Jes jumped. Why was he following her?

"Nope. I'm going to sit." She migrated towards an empty round lunch table."Raush was almost human today." She searched for anything to say.

"He's okay," Nate said. "I've gone in for help and he's pretty good one on one."

"Maybe he just doesn't like being in front of everybody. I wouldn't," she said. How could she get rid of Nate? Her mind was blank and banalities dribbled out of her mouth. Why wouldn't he take the hint and leave her alone? He was okay and she didn't want to do it in front of him. She was an idiot but she didn't have to drag him down too.

"He probably just hates life. I think teachers get tired of kids," Nate said. "We're such assholes. Look at Galen. He's got everything in his corner, star athlete, money, good looks, and he acts like a jerk." Nate was babbling, she smiled. He was kind of an idiot too.

"I think he broke up with Suzaan today. Crappy timing."

"Oh I wondered why she was crying," Nate said.

"BAMM! BAMM! BAMM!

The sound reverberated in the vast empty commons and Jes covered her ears against the noise. She clutched at her purse and and touched the gun to reassure herself that it hadn't gone off as Nate hauled her from the table.

Nate was scanning the empty commons. "Who is shooting?!"

The End of Days. Now, here it was and she hadn't even started it.

"It wasn't me," she said which sounded ridiculous even as it came out of her mouth.

"BAMM! BAMM! BAMM!

Nate dragged her to behind one of the large pillars.

"I think it's Galen." Nate said. "What does he think he's doing?"

Nate pulled a long thin wicked looking knife out of his boot and shoved Jes behind him. Emboldened, Jes took the sleek and deadly gun out of her purse.

"Whoa, you win," Nate's eyes widened.

"Should we rush him?" Jes whispered.

"Let's parlay." Nate pulled a white paper napkin off the condiment table, stood up and waved it.

"Hey parlay!" he yelled.

"What the fuck is parlay?" Yelled Galen across the commons.

"Like from Pirates of the Caribbean. We talk and you don't shoot us." He said.

"Geez, even I've seen that," Jes muttered to Nate.

"Okay, just for a minute though. I've got a lot of shit to do today." Galen laughed. Nate set off towards him, the knife hanging down by his leg.

"Wait!" Jes ran up behind him and together, they walked across the commons to where Galen stood. He held the gun on them, dark and heavy in a shaking hand.

"What's going on, Galen?" Nate's voice was low and calm. Jes held onto his left arm.

Galen took a step back and Jes saw the gun waver in his hand.

"Aw, nothing much, you know, shooting up the school, followed by suicide. The usual."

"Sounds messy." Nate cringed.

"Hey, Jes, you want to join me?" Galen motioned to her gun. "Sounds like your little life is just one step off of paradise too. Sorry Nate, a knife just doesn't cut it. You can't be in the Massacre Club.

Only those whose lives truly suck," He laughed but Jes would tell it was forced.

"You want to talk about raw suckage? Fuck you." Nate pushed up his sleeves.

Jes leaned in and gasped. Like tiny railroad tracks, the cuts marched up his arm as high as she could see.

"Not the cool dude everyone thinks you are," Galen lowered the gun and ran a finger up Nate's arm.

"Don't touch them, they itch and it makes me want to cut more." Nate slid his sleeve down.

"I think it makes you even more of a badass. We're just three little damaged packages of goods, aren't we? How many do you think we can take out?"

"Wait," said Jes, "How the hell do you qualify? You've got a golden spoon in your mouth, and you're a moron besides."

"Okay, how's this? I'm the star of my dad's own personal memoir. He wanted to play ball so I have to be the great quarterback. He wants a blond princess, I find one. I don't even have the stones to tell him I'd rather go with Nate than Suzaan. I hate football. I have no idea what I want to do with my life, I mean HIS life. I broke up with Suzaan today. She hates my guts. Maybe you can take her to Homecoming Nate."

Nate's smile was tight. "I was trying to ask Jes before you started this shitstorm. Now, they'll probably cancel it."

Jes sucked in air. The hand with the gun flew to her face. Her first date. Almost date. What the fuck.

"You think they'll cancel the dance?" She asked.

"I am pretty positive it will be cancelled," said Nate.

"Sorry I fucked up your little love life," Galen said.

"Galen," Jes stepped in front of Nate, "Did anyone see you with the gun besides us?"

"I don't think so. It was pretty empty when I came in. Like my life. I was just going to shoot whatever heros show up. And look, it's just you two losers in life. Hey, there's security footage." He pointed the gun at a camera high on the wall.

"Those are fake," Nate said. "Too expensive for real ones."

"Come on," Jes slid her gun back in her oversized cloth purse. "Give me your gun and the knife. Now!" Jes hissed. Galen hesitated then dropped his gun into her bag. Nate grinned and slid the knife in.

"Let's get back to physics class."

"What is going on in that red headed brain of yours, Jes?" Galen shook his head. Jes turned on him, grabbing his shirt front with her small hands.

"No way are you fucking up the first date I've ever had." She rounded on Nate, "I don't have any money for dinner or the ticket."

"I got that covered. I work in my dad's machine shop doing maintenance to earn money."

"Why isn't anyone stopping decorating?" Asked Galen, looking around.

"Doesn't seem like they heard the shots," Nate said as they moved through the crowd.

"Probably down here it sounded like the janitor slamming the lunch tables up for cleaning," Jes said.

"Plus it's really loud in the hall," Galen said, smiling. There was music playing with a dance beat.

Nate shook his head, but followed her. Galen trailed behind. Jes stopped before the door.

She used the t-shirt under her hoodie to polish both guns and the knife, using the boys as shields.

"Is this gun registered?" She asked.

"No, it's from my dad's collection of unregistered firearms," he smirked.

"Ready?" She looked from one to the other.

"Wait, what are we supposed to do?" Nate whispered.

"Look freaked out. We have to get the active shooter plan started. You know, where we all beserk out any door and run amok through town so they can't shoot us."

"How is that going to work if no one heard anything?" Galen said.

"There'll be bullet holes and then a search," said Jes. "We can't afford to be searched."

Jes swung open the door.

"Back already?" Raush peered at them. He sat in the deserted room, grading quizzes.

"Shooting in the commons. I didn't see anyone but I heard shots. We were in the hall and we figured it was safer here."

"Oh my God. Everyone run. I'll check the hall." He moved quickly, his white lab coat flapping.

Jes grabbed the phone on the wall and hit the intercom button, "Active shooter in the commons. This is not a drill. Active shooter in the commons." She hung up the phone and headed towards the door at the end of the hall. People were screaming and running ahead of her and Nate grabbed her hand.

"Where are you guys going?" Asked Galen, running to catch up to them.

"I'm thinking of escaping towards the riverwalk, where the river is really deep." Jes said.

"I'll go with," Nate said "I have something I'd like to ask you, properly like. Try and be surprised. Although they'll probably cancel the dance. We can go have pie or something."

"Good. I don't have a dress anyway."

"Think they'll cancel the game?" grinned Galen.

"Wouldn't surprise me a bit," said Nate.

Urban Horror

A murky haze hung in the air around the decrepit house, as if squeezed out by the houses around it. To its right, a breath of space, a smudge of green where the floating miasma concentrated. A short, ancient forged metal fence that guaranteed tetanus snugged inside a higher gray chain link that felt more at home in the struggling neighborhood.

"We're home, kiddos," their mother danced up the cracked gray pavers that led to the gothic revival wreck in her high topped Keds and worn jeans, not just retro but vintage.

Arun's eyes darted to find something good, anything. A tired, graceless rectangle painted a faded, hideous green presented as their new home. Dark shutters, at awkward angles, hung on the façade. Four dingy white pillars struggled to support the roof overhang. They formed a dizzying series of parallelograms across the slanted porch. A turret hung off the one side of the second story, as if clinging desperately to hold on to the worthless structure. Just another single family row house streaming a segment from the heart of the city like legs of a diseased spider.

"Pile of whack," Cantor pronounced over the scream music banging out of her ear buds. A terminally angry 13, nothing was good in her life, reflected her brother Arun, a more mature 16. She wore only black which accented her painful thinness and her dark brown eyes were rimmed in black, smudging down her cheeks and reddening her eyes by the end of the day so she looked more in need of a hug than a cause.

"Turret is mine," she claimed, looking up at the house. Arun would rather have a view over the smoky plot of empty land than the neighbor's windows. "Unless mother takes it," she amended.

They settled into their house, Cantor in the lopsided turret, Arun across the hall overlooking what turned out to be an unkempt graveyard and their mother in a more spacious room in the back of the second floor with an attached bathroom.

Cantor attempted to shut her door, but the door frame didn't coincide with the door. She jammed it as close as possible to shut. Arun left his door open and moved the desk to the window so he could stare out the window at the graveyard. He left his lights off to improve visibility.

The glowing tip of a cigarette resolved in the haze inside the fence around the graveyard; a darker form within the misty shadows, large and bulky in ragged clothes. A bum.

How dangerous would it be to talk to the man? He was inside the double fence of the cemetery and Arun would be on the outside. He bet he could outrun some old smoker, for he felt the man was old, perhaps ancient. He walked soft-footed down the stairs but heard Cantor's door wrench open, anyway.

"What's the dilly, doofus?"

"There's some crusty goombah out in the cemetery next door. Thought I'd go see what his deal is."

"God, you need a keeper." She shadowed him till they were noses to the fence.

"Hello," Arun whispered. He felt Cantor tighten next to him.

"Hello," it said, sucking the cigarette until it glowed white.

Another thing formed beside it, more polished, less foul. It bore a resemblance to their father, who deserted them when they were just toddlers. Arun barely remembered him, but Cantor, three years younger, claimed vivid memories. Her breath sucked in.

"So you're the cool kids in the house," the dad-like thing said. He was dressed in jeans and a white t-shirt. Looked about 30, mature but not old yet.

"Where have you been?" Spat Cantor, forcing her face into the damp fence.

"Here, where I've always been. You'll be gone before the month is out, they always are," he said sadly.

"If you're here, I'm staying," Cantor said.

"Okay, but first we've got to ditch the golem," He jerked a thumb at the dark form in the ragged clothes, smoking.

"How?" she demanded.

"Simple, prick your finger and you can change places with him. Be with me all the time. Good times, trust me." The edges of his silhouette vibrated.

The thing made Arum recoil. Cantor whipped out a safety pin out and stabbed her finger. The blood was dark but vibrant, like a living organism with a fluttering heartbeat. Arun squeezed his hand over her finger. "No."

He slid out his pocket knife and sliced his arm at mid elbow. A bright wash of blood sluiced down his arm. He and Cantor had never been close. But something was terrifyingly wrong about this creature. He might lose himself, but he would protect Cantor. They never saw eye to eye, had never bonded as siblings, but he could save her and he would.

The frayed, dusty figure next to the dad-thing, laughed a deep hacking laugh that dissolved into a cough.

"I still have some grace left." He reached out a gray hand and wrapped it around Arun's wound. Arun hung onto Cantor's finger and they looked like an old playground game of Red Rover. Enormous wings pushed through the thing's tattered clothing and where before he looked weak, he expanded with unbounded power.

Arun felt a searing glow in his arm claw its way up to his elbow. He felt wonder and his skin blistering. His flesh pulled back from the thing's hand but regenerated pink and new underneath.

The dad-like thing hissed and slid back into the cooler shadows of the cemetery. His lovely smooth face crinkled and cracked and his frame fractalled into writhing snakes of ash. Cantor gasped and tried to flee, but Arun squeezed onto her hand tighter as his new flesh solidified.

"Beat it, demon. It was too easy anyway," the winged creature said to the snake things. "Kids, these days are too needy."

"Thank you," gasped Arun, "but why? You're a frickin' angel. You could have been free."

"I'd be reassigned. And there are worse gigs in all of heaven and earth. Trust me."

Chickens don't do it for me.

Voodoo again. DJ

One after another, through the dark swamp, the few of the faithful slid into his hut like shadows passing the bright moon. Could the Hougan help her son? Could the Hougan ease the pain? Should they move or stay, Hougan? His once bright golden eyes, the mark of the High Priest, had faded to the pale yellow of a peeled potato.

He did what he could for those few who sought him out in the old ways, comforting the people who still kept to the sacred path.

He didn't do all that much, he admitted to himself as he half listened to the man before him. His role was mostly to give advice. The powerful magik that was the cornerstone of their religion was in short supply for the poor. The younger people ignored him and made their own way without the comfort of Voodoo.

The pain of age crawled down his back and he wondered what the people would do when he was gone. Would they travel to the larger port city for a Hougan? It would be expensive and he doubted any other priest would accept their meager offerings as he did. During the day, he worked the fields as any other man did to make his living. He supposed it was hard to see him sweating under the beating sun and then imagine him as a conduit of the powerful magik during the full moon.

The man before him grew silent. It was time.

With a quick practiced motion, he twisted the chicken's neck from its body.

The old man in front of him shook as the blood spattered his face. Not the slight vibration of a chill but the bone shaking rattle of the believer. He left a few coins and slipped out with the chicken. Supper tomorrow, the Hougan thought.

He waited but no one claimed the spot. That must be it for tonight. It was good; he was tired.

The Hougan sighed and began the laborious process of getting up. Pain was eating him from the inside. It could be put at bay only so long before it took him. He wouldn't have to worry about a successor for long. It was sad but not many would be disappointed.

The old ways were slipping away like the shadow of a bird high in the sky.

A cloud walked past the moon, plunging the hut into darkness. The Hougan paused, waiting for it to pass but the moonlight did not return and a dark mountain in the form of a man with burning eyes appeared in the seat. The Hougan could see precious metals glinting on his gleaming arms and legs.

"Are you a true believer?" The voice like the scraping of stones.

"I am," he whispered, a tear jerked down his face.

The man pulled two smokes out of the darkness and handed one to the Hougan. "So few really do believe."

The Hougan's hand shook as the thing lit both smokes and handed one to him. The sweet smoke curled around them. The Hougan's consciousness began to float like fine ash as the powerful drug took hold of him.

"What we need," it drew in the smoke, but never released it, he noticed, "Is a new, powerful Hougan. Someone to bring the sacrifices back and restore respect to its proper level." He leaned towards the Hougan and the air compressed between them. Fear clutched at the Hougan's chest and his breath wheezed.

"I do miss a good sacrifice," his laughter was like a rumbling storm before the rain. "Chickens just don't do it for me."

The Hougan thought about his life as he floated above his seated body. He'd had a good woman who bore him a daughter but no sons. "My daughter," he whispered.

"Yes, the one who ran away. I've kept a watch on her for you. She's one of my favorites. You'd like to see her one more time and know that she's fine? I can do that for you, for one of my true believers." The thing nodded. "She's everything we could have hoped for."

A cold wind ripped through the hut. Not the wonderful cool breeze in a stifling heat but a searing cold rapier that bit the skin.

"Why, here she is now."

Another darkness moved through the door. Slim and quick with long swirling hair the color of night. The Hougan wept as he caught a glimpse of her fierce golden eyes and ebony face just as the knife plunged down.

Jazz Man

The sweltering New Orleans night wraps the three young men in an envelope of warmth as they work their swagger through the ruined city. Heavy with moisture, the cloying air suffuses them with anger; anger at life, anger at the city, anger at everything. Fear is their ocean, and the feeding is exceptional in this hurricane-broken city, vulnerable to degradation.

Clutching beer cans that sweat seed pearls of moisture down their hands. Their faces silvered by the fat moon hanging over the crescent city. Forlorn notes of a trumpet waft to them, dancing along the streamers of white fog rising from the broken sidewalks.

Drawn like yarn from a skein, they move towards the intricate syncopation until they see him. An old man, ancient, almost indistinguishable from the muddy rock he perches on beside a rusted out fountain.

His skin has a sheen in the moonlight. Is he creole? black, mulatto? He is all of them at once and none, but there is a subtle power, an underlying strength that no freak weather phenomenon can destroy. The men can only see prey, and a smile fleets across their faces. One yells out, "Hey, old man," but it drops like wet tissue into the space.

He might have been part of the rock, except for the blur of moving fingers on his trumpet. Intricate tunings drift softly from the bell like strands of silver lacing through the hot air.

Confused, they stand before him. The music traps them for a moment, evoking images of the damaged city and the desperate sorrow of its people. Pain floods their minds. They shake their heads to dislodge the visions, preferring to dwell in the primitive part of their brains.

One throws the rest of his tepid beer on the elder. The music evolves, engorges like the hurricane swell that devastated the streets and buildings just days ago. A few barks of laughter from the others as the brew drips down the old man's face onto his wet pants and shirt. Flood loess, the finest of silt, crawls up his pant legs like clutching hands. His shoes are worn by trudging through flood waters from the surge.

But his music is filled with broken promises so sweet their teeth ache, longing so fierce their guts tighten and promise; the promise of renewal.

"We're the new kings here, Jazz Man, Soul Man," the bravest dances a few lewd moves, grinding hips. "We're going to tear this city apart, starting with you." New courage flows through the group, electric, and they advance on the old man.

The music fades and he shakes his head in regret, glittering droplets of beer spatter to the ground. The old man sucks in on the battered horn, pulling them off their feet and into the horn. Swallows them; swallows them whole, their dark twitching souls screaming at the precipice of hell.

The Jazz Man, soul of the city, tears running freely down his seamed face, plays a dark dirge.

Black Gold

*I have a degree in geology. Always on the lookout for a dinosaur reprise.
DJ*

When the dinosaurs reappeared, they looked more like miniature lizards than something from the Mesozoic era. They were cute and colorful and the conservative media made a big deal out of finding a new species. Climate change was for losers.

So we kept right on pumping hydrocarbons into the atmosphere like the world was going to keep on keepin' the same forever. The little buggers reproduced at an alarming rate and soon were everywhere. Even in Fort Stockton, Texas, where there wasn't much except oil wells as far as the eye can see, you had to watch where you put your boot or you'd squish one.

Evolution had done a fast break and the next new species to make an appearance was not so cute. They had wings for one thing. Leathery and shiny like something out of a horror movie. And teeth. Sweet Mother of God. They had rows of vicious, flesh ripping teeth. They were bigger than the Neosaurs (what they named the little lizardy ones). They named them Dentapods for their most prominent attribute.

The Dentapods hunted down the Neosaurs with a terrifying pack mentality. They killed them not just for food but for some other compulsion. I'd say sport but it was more than that. Strewn guts covered the roads, blood soaking into the sand.

I guess the Neosaurs reproduced so fast because otherwise, they would have been extinct, again. Attacks from the flyers came out of the blinding sun and they tore those little guys apart. And they didn't give a hoot if their wings were close enough to cut you as they dove past. They didn't care one whit.

When it came to food, they seemed to really prefer the Neos but weren't adverse to picking off cats and dogs and the odd toddler who wandered out of doors. The Neos became adept at hiding, learning to duck and cover whenever a shadow touched them. When the Dentas ran out of easy prey, their black shiny eyes started looking at us. Really looking.

Everyone found a reason to stay inside around that time and hoped the military would get off its big old behind and save us. And they tried. You had to give 'em that. But most of the regular military stuff didn't work against the Dentapods. Not tanks or airplanes or bombs.

The Dentapods weren't stupid either. Once they realized we were trying to kill them they decided to kill us right back. And they were better at it than we were by a long ways. They slaughtered the army of conventional warfare like it was a choir practice.

By the time we ramped up the shooting war, the Dentas figured out how to ambush squads and cut their losses. And we learned that pretty much only a direct hit to the brain would take them out of action. Direct hit. Our military is more "lots of bullets, good percentage of hits" type. It Really didn't work out well for them. Or should I say us. Sooner rather than later, there wasn't much of a military left anymore.

The scientists dug in and found out anything that would poison them would poison us too. People all over the world were wringing their hands and praying for salvation. But this is Texas and that ain't the way we do things around these parts.

Word went out from Colonel Hazard through the church telephone calling tree. He called everyone in. We'd all been waiting for it, we just hadn't known it. He wasn't a Colonel any more but nobody ever called him anything but. He did some really scary, heroic things in the last war overseas but they were so secret, no one would talk about them, even if they knew.

One thing was for sure, the man was one badass. He nodded at you, and you felt eight feet tall. Women sighed when he walked past. He wore a tan Stetson and well worn boots. He had family money from oil and lived in a big fenced in spread on the west side of Fort Stockton. But the well cut suits didn't fool anyone; he was a hard, hard man.

The church was packed. Even the Jewish guys who had an art store in town came. I can't think of anyone who wasn't there. When it came time for the homily, he and the pastor both stood up. After a moment the pastor sat right back down as the Colonel took the pulpit.

He looked out over the people of his community and he showed the great leadership ability that had given him rank in the military. Fans stopped waving, babies stopped fussing, waiting for the man to speak.

"These abominations from Hell have to be stopped. They threaten to take over our world, make it their own. I've word through channels that a new, larger species has been discovered. Or maybe it's better to say they've discovered us and are spreading rapidly. My sources say this new, larger, deadly threat will be here in two weeks at the most. Now, I don't know about you, neighbor, but I've never fancied being part of someone else's food chain. Oil runs through my veins, just like it does yours. No one's taking my land from me and I'm not much on running, neither. " There was scattered laughter at the very thought.

I know we have come to rely on our military to protect us. Our military is gone, torn apart by these night terrors. We turned in our guns like good citizens when they passed the No Death on Our Streets law a couple of years ago. I also know that like me, you've all got one good gun you've designated as a family heirloom to keep at home for protection. Well, I for one, hope you kept plenty of ammo for that firearm.

"I'm saying now's the time to clean that gun. We survived the Alamo. We survived the Democrats and by God, we'll survive these things." He paused and ran a blinding white handkerchief across his brow.

"Tomorrow at noon, I'll be at the compound with as many of you as are willing and able— men, women and children. Anyone who can shoot and has a gun. And we're going to clean these bastards out. I've got enough food and water for as long as we need. Bring whatever you need to bring.

We don't rely on anyone but kin and neighbor, never have. We take care of our own problems. Why? Because that's what Texans do. Till tomorrow, my friends."

And he walked out down the center aisle. People rose and followed just like the ushers had dismissed them, row by row.

Greener Pastures

A friend asked me to write this from a prompt. Not my fault. DJ

Amur Not Nimble seemed to materialize out of a grey cloud of smoke near the heavy metal door of the bar. The giant made no noise but some primitive survival antennae caused the other patrons of the Rusty Nail bar to swivel and take note of his arrival. Not enough to challenge, but to show that he was on their radar. A few stared at his face, then looked away.

The Rusty Nail catered to the gritiest of the lower eschelon on the planet Meridae, miners and the least desirable male whores sat at the rugged metal tables, waiting for trade or some higher ups slumming. Or the entertainment of a fight.

Amur raised his remaining eye head to the bar keep and made a sign for "two." Two whiskeys were set before him. He didn't frequent the Rusty Nail often but Amur wasn't someone likely to be forgotten. A heavy flap of skin hung over his forehead, inexpertly sewn back to cover the gaping hole where his eye had been gouged out by another miner trying to scalp him. Long time ago, another lifetime.

He'd earned his nickname, "Not Nimble" when one of his legs had been torn off at the hip by an earth grinder in the mine. Losing a limb was common enough that they were able to stop the bleeding in time to save his life. Pity that. His metal peg prosthesis was compensation for the accident by the Company.

He still experienced excruciating pain as if it had just happened, but it was a lucky thing in Amur's mind because the accident was his ticket out of the prison. They released him from his sentence but where would a misshapen lump of flesh like him go? One place was as good as another until you died. So he remained in the mines, sweeping filings in exchange for a tiny room, food with the inmates and a couple of shill a month. It wasn't much, but enough for Amur's simple needs.

He took his drinks and made his way to the Shill Room. It was the only private place he could think of. A place for perversion but not for Amur tonight.

The door was closed, the light said it was busy. He was pleased he had thought to come here. Only place a man could get some privacy. He sat at a small round table, dwarfing it with his huge elbows. He drank the first fiery drink and then the other, ignoring the entreaties of the whores.

The door opened and a wiry man slid out. The door continued its mechanical opening and another man, thin and shaky, staggered away, a dirty sheet wrapped around his torso, blood spotting the back of it.

Amur went into the Shill room, past the jeers of onlookers. His one eyed stare silenced them. He put the shill in the slot and closed the door softly. Another shill put a clean sheet on the bed.

Then, he reached into a deep pocket, unbuttoning the cover that held the pocket closed, away from quick fingers. He pulled out something wrapped in the cheap mining canvas used everywhere on the planet. He gently unwrapped it, marvelling anew at how such a beautiful object had fallen into his path.

Amur had been taking out garbage, as he did every day to earn his bed and shills. The bag of trash seemed abnormally heavy. Picking through it, he'd found the dead man, balled up like so much refuse. Searching his pockets yielded nothing, but when death had released the man's bowels, this gem had come out and ended up in his pants, sparkling like glitter among the feces. Amur washed it off and hid it quickly before anyone took an interest.

More than just a pretty gem, there was life in it. The colors swirled inside, writhing. There was no one for Amur to ask for an opinion on what to do with such a life-changing find. He had no friends. He feared his room at the mine might be monitored. Just the suggestion of him having something interesting would be worth his life.

The thing was slippery smooth and he rubbed it like he'd heard in some fable from his distant childhood, but nothing happened. He wondered what to do. He hated that the thing had given him hope. Hope for another, better life evaporated as he held it before him. He'd thought he could sell it for a spaceship and travel the galaxy.

He'd been born on a green planet. Not every planet was choked in its own dust like this one. He knew they were out there. He could find somewhere far away from the prying eyes that were fascinated by his face and then frightened of him. It'd been a long time since hope had wrenched his heart like this. A tear fell onto the pretty thing. Just a visit to a pawn shop with such a treasure might hasten his death. To hope was a trap.

In a fit of frustration, he threw the stone against the wall of the Shill Room. It dashed into a million scintillating rainbows that darted around the room. The giant stepped back as a fresh young man in a clean, expensive tunic walked from the wall and sat on the bed.

It was him, as a young man before he'd been sent to Meridae as a prisoner on a trumped up charge by his uncle.

"So, why am I here?" The young man spoke. He was tall, broad and well formed from years of living well on his home planet. He had

Amur's height if not yet his thickness.

"Can you hear me, boy?"

"Of course, I can. This is the most realistic dream I've ever had." Amur's people believed in the portents of dreams.

"It's not a dream," Amur said, "I'm your future."

"No, my father just died and now I run the family business," the man-boy shook his soft long locks.

"You idiot. Listen to me. I don't know how long this magic lasts."

"Magic? This is real?" He leaned forward and plucked at the gray sheet.

"Yes, our uncle framed us for embezzlement and sent you, me, to this hell hole Meridae."

The boy leaned back, thoughtful. "I can see he might be capable of that, but what can I do?"

"KIll him" the giant ground his meaty hands together.

"Then, I'll still get sent here but for murder." The boy argued.

"Poison? The apothecary might help. Uncle is a brutal and unloved master."

"I think I have a better idea," the lad stood up. "He has an ugly daughter he adores. She's desperately in need of a suitor. Perhaps it's time I chose a wife. Who says the grass is greener in a neighbor's pasture. Who can know for sure? Perhaps we'll have a love to span the ages." The good looking young man stood, brushed off some imaginary dirt from the cot and walked to the wall where he'd come.The rainbow of colors seemed to shimmer and then fade to ash as he added, "Thank you and see you soon."

After the 15 minutes were up, the door swung open automatically and to the amazement of all, the room was empty.

Deja vu

Bad choices? Good choices? Hard to say. DJ

The sound was unmistakable. Even though Tali never heard a car hit a person before, she knew what it was. She turned as one small gym shoe, white as a sunflower seed, arced into the air. The tiny, boneless body windmilled after the shoe. The child had been behind her in the crosswalk.

It could have been Tali, a few seconds earlier, walking home from high school with her heavy book bag. Just stupid luck it was the next kid. Another proof that her life was worth something. The good Lord intended her to make a difference. Maybe be a physician like that woman in the movie in class today.

The little sista was almost sure dead. She should go check, though.

Before she could make her legs move, the squealing of metal tore the air as the car that had hit the little girl, careened off an SUV.

A man's body rammed through the windshield like a spear and landed on the sidewalk right in front of her, almost on her shoe. A long ragged gash in his chest filled with blood and Talia's vision narrowed to a point while her stomach flipped. She gritted her teeth and shook herself. Maybe this was the Lord's test to see if she could be a doctor.

The man's chest had a deep fissure from the collarbone to the belly button. His guts glistened and pieces of white bone were scattered through the hole like dice. The seam filled endlessly with blood. He was probably gonna die but she could maybe keep him alive until the ambulance came.

She knelt in the broken glass and pressed her hands together as if in prayer, on either side of the rift to close the opening. The blood bubbled up like warm bread dough pushing through her brown fingers.

The shattered glass from the windshield bit into her knees, but she kept pressure on to hold the two ragged edges of the wound together.

People gathered and established their own periphery on the grass on the other side of the smoking car. Probably didn't want to get involved in anyone else's business. People were like that and that was okay. Being a hero wasn't for everyone. Blood covered her hands, but she kept on the pressure.

Everyone stood there, stupid, but not her. If she was meant to be a physician, this would be the moment that decided her future for her. Her arms ached with the strain of keeping the pressure on. Whatever she became, gonna get there by hard work and scholarships. Not gonna get a baby in her like some of the girls. She wasn't having any of what those boys were selling. She'd had enough to last a lifetime. Yeah, her brown eyes were nice and her hair was soft. It was gonna take more than sugar to derail her life. She'd had a rough enough start without adding to it.

When she was seven years old, Tali was in charge of herself while her mama slept from second shift at the grocery and third cleaning hotel rooms part time.

A dark man with a whispery voice like crinkling paper, lived down the street and had a nose for children who weren't under anyone's watch. He'd found her fast enough and told her he'd kill her if she told. Those two years were a nightmare she re-lived every night of her life.

He'd disappeared one day after complaining that she was developing too fast and it was unattractive to him. It was her best birthday present ever even if it wasn't on her birthday. Tali never told anyone, not even her mama. What could anyone do to fix it? Now, she was old enough she could defend herself.

The blood from the man's chest seemed to be slowing. Tali wondered what was wrong inside his body. Was it his heart? The sweat ran into her eyes as she struggled to keep him alive.

She'd vowed to make a difference in someone's life, the way she always prayed someone would appear back then to rescue her. Saving this guy would be the start of making her mark in the world.

She pushed all her weight into keeping his wound closed, heard him grunt in pain.

"Hold on, help is coming," Tali muttered. Sirens wailed in the distance.

"Thank you," the man whispered.

That voice. Tali's hand slipped off him in the blood. Her breath caught deep in her gut and she couldn't hear anything as if her ears were muffled in a pillow. The searing pain in her chest brought her right back to being seven years old. His voice, that whispering rasp, was in her nightmares every night, replaying like a scratchy recording. The shaking began and she couldn't keep her hands still. Blood flowed out of his wound like a river overflowing its banks.

Tali took a deep breath. She wasn't that girl anymore, vowed to never be afraid like that again. She wiped her bloody hands on the clean sleeve of his shirt and stood up. Maybe her gift was to make it so no other little girl had to be afraid like that. She brushed the glass off of the knees of her jeans.

Maybe he deserved to live for some reason in God's big plan. Wasn't her call. God would save him, if she wanted to. Tali was just a kid walking home from school.

Making a difference in the world was important, Tali picked up her heavy backpack. Not everyone could be a hero. Only those who were strong. She was strong, she realized. Strong enough to make the hard choice and do the right thing.

Freedom morning

Retelling of a true event. DJ

The nineteen men crowded into the jail cell, accused of killing a white police chief, David Hennessey. They stood shoulder to shoulder without enough room to sit or sleep and had stood all night. They acted with dignity as if a night in jail was nothing to them but Gaspare could smell the acid fear. And no one was more afraid than he was. At fourteen years old, Gaspare fought to be a man like his father who stood next to him. His whole body trembled as he stood listening to the rumble of anger from a crowd outside the barred window. It came and went, each wave of noise grew louder until the walls shook with it.

Dawn hovered at the edge of the horizon; he felt it although he could not see it. If today was a normal day, he and his father would be on their way to the market to sell fruit. They missed one day of work already and now two.

Yesterday, he and his father were acquitted of the murder along with four other men. Three additional men were cleared when the jury couldn't decide. He didn't understand "acquitted" but his father whispered it meant freedom.

The rabble outside roared like an injured beast when the verdicts reached them. It was so loud that the judge couldn't continue and they were herded back to the crowded cell. As they scurried from the courtroom building through the alley and back to the jail, people screamed at them. He'd never seen so many people in his life.

The anger on their faces made them look inhuman and they yelled horrible things. He wasn't a "nigger" or a "brute." Where did these names come from? He'd hoped to be released but the police said it was too dangerous. They said the mob outside numbered in the thousands.

When he got to the door of the cell, he gasped for air and his breathing became ragged. His chest hurt and he stopped to catch his breath. Someone shoved him and sweat rose on his chest and face. He struggled to get out of the cell and his father held him, calmed him. Eventually, the darkness in front of his eyes faded and he was able to stand calmly.

He remembered when his father had told them they were going to the City of New Orleans for new opportunities. How excited he'd been. He and father sent money home each week, proud to care for their family back home. Would his mother be proud of him today, in a jail cell accused of murder?

The uniformed man closed the cell door but Thomas noticed he didn't lock it. And why should he? They were all innocent of the murder. Yesterday, the police rounded them up like cattle at the market and didn't tell them why or where they were going. Nineteen men were as many as could fit in the wagon or they would have taken more. A boom shook dust out of the ceiling down upon them as Gaspare and the men in the cell held their collective breaths.

His father gripped his arm roughly and moved him out of the cell. He found a supply closet in the hallway and shoved him in, closing the door after him.

Gaspare heard the screaming hoard streaming into the jail. The floors shook and he squeezed himself into a ball and prayed for his father and the other men. His breath became labored. This time there were no kind hands to hold him. His vision narrowed to a single point and he lost consciousness.

He woke in darkness and whimpered until he realized he was still in the closet. He cracked open the door and saw a pool of blood on the floor of the cell. He stumbled out of the jail, the only person in a serene world and made his way back to the tent where he and his father slept.

At the cross street, he saw them. Eleven of the men he'd shared a cell with, shared every day of life in America at the market. They hung from ropes, still in the cool morning. They'd been beaten and their faces were barely recognizable. He saw his father, limbs at awkward angles and his face a red pulp.

A woman walked past him and spit on the ground in front of him. "Dago," she said.

The largest mass lynching in America was March 14, 1891 when 11 innocent Italian Americans, some already tried and acquitted were killed by an angry mob for the death of a police chief. Lynching is more brutal than hanging. In hanging, the neck snaps and death is instantaneous. In lynching, the person is pulled up from the ground, struggling for air and slowly suffocates.

As a result of the lynchings, Italy cut off diplomatic relations with the United States, raising rumors of war. Theodore Roosevelt, not yet president, wrote to his sister: "Monday we dined at the Camerons; various dago[1] diplomats were present, all much wrought up by the lynching of the Italians in New Orleans. Personally I think it rather a good thing, and said so." The killing of the police chief, David Hennessy introduced the word "Mafia" to the American public. Gaspare Marchesi, the boy who survived by hiding in the jail while his father was lynched, was awarded $5,000 in damages in 1893 after suing the city of New Orleans.

In April, 2019, the mayor of New Orleans offered an apology.

---

1. https://en.wikipedia.org/wiki/Dago_(slur)

Making a Difference

"Your offer is appreciated, Ryan. We admire your resolve to make a difference but we have selected other candidates to be featured in the Ribbons For Cancer calendar." Ryan tossed the letter across the table to his mother. "I guess I don't have that "cute" cancer look they're searching for. No sense in applying for next year." He stalked to his room.

"Ryan!" His mother sobbed. All she did was cry. At least he'd tried to make a difference with the 13 years he'd been alloted.

"I should have gone with my own calendar. Only problem is it would be a half year calendar by the time I'm done," he muttered, looking at the corkboard wall of refusal letters.

He'd written the FBI body farm, teaching hospitals even the Children's museum and no one wanted his cancer ridden corpse. No takers.

"I just want to make some kind of difference before I die. Even the organ donor people said no."

"You've made a difference to me," his mother stood in the doorway, sniffling. The ache inside him felt like a hollowed out pumpkin. Thirteen years on this Earth and nothing to show for it.

"You got another letter." She held out the slim envelope to him. Maybe one of the testing labs he'd written to could use his tissues for research. Ryan snatched the letter and tore it open.

"Crap. Eighth grade birthday party. Lame." Ryan tossed it aside. He had more important things to do with the time he had left. He just had to figure out what.

His mother picked up the invitation. "You should go. Enjoy yourself. Maybe a new idea will come to you. You could make a friend." Her lips were pursed so tight, he wondered her lips weren't bleeding.

"It's a pity invite," he scoffed.

"So what? Maybe you'll touch someone's life while you're there." She stabbed a pin through the invite, attaching it onto the wall. "And it wouldn't hurt you to have some fun. Just be careful, you know what the doctor said."

Ryan glanced at the invitation. A Halloween party. Should he go as "cured"? Be careful. The doctor had explained it in gruesome detail.

"Ryan, you have a rare side effect of cancer, hemophilia. Do you know what that is?" The eyes peered over his dirty glasses at Ryan as if he were an interesting bug.

"Yeah, if I get cut, I bleed to death."

"Not just that. If you hit your head or your hand too hard, there can be catastrophic internal bleeding. If you cut yourself, chances are you'll be okay if it is shallow. Deeper, definitely call 911, let them know your condition." He smiled at Ryan as if he wasn't dying.

"Maybe I'll go." He told his mom just to get her off his back. Her smile rewarded him. "I think I actually know this kid."

*****

"Here, we spiked the punch." Jerry handed him a plastic cup. "Oh wait, you can have stuff like that, right?"

"Yeah," Ryan sipped the pink drink, grimacing at the bitter taste. "Uck"

"Vodka's an acquired taste," Jerry smacked him on the back.

Ryan winced, thinking about internal bleeding. Dying at a party would be more interesting than laying in hospice.

He sipped the drink again. What would happen when it mixed with all the other crap the doctors had him taking? It burned his throat and his head spun, but not unpleasantly.

Jerry slipped away into the crowd. Ryan watched him. He knocked on a door. A bedroom door? It cracked and Ryan could see the room was lit by candles, a girl he knew peeked out and then admitted Jerry.

Ryan knocked gently on the door. Jerry opened the door a crack. "Hey Ryan."

"What's going on?"

Ryan glanced back and then opened the door to admit him. "We're an edgy group. You know?"

"No, what does edgy mean?" Ryan said looking around the dim room. No one met his eye.

"We're cutters, Ryan," the girl whose name he couldn't recall said to him.

"Cutters?"

"We cut ourselves," Jerry took Ryan's arm and drew him into the candle-lit glow of the room. The door shut behind him.

"Jesus, why?" Ryan asked. He looked at the proffered arm of the girl and saw the parallel slices that marched up her arm like stitches.

"It feels good." She told him. He watched in a horror of fascination as she took a new razor blade and drew it across her arm, above the crook. She hissed and closed her eyes as the blood seeped out of the inch long cut.

"Is this healthy at all?" Ryan wondered aloud.

The girl shrugged her thin shoulders. "We like it. It isn't that bad. Not as bad as smoking. Nobody's forcing you to." She turned away.

Ryan felt an invisible curtain fall between him and the group of cutters. They bent over their arms and busied themselves with slicing their tender flesh open.

Ryan turned away. It was wrong, it revolted him but what could he do about it?

Make a difference, he thought grimly. He would make a difference.

"Give me the razor," he said quietly.

"Dude!" Jerry patted him on the back. "One of us." Murmurs of welcome ran around the room and the girl handed him a new razor blade, unwrapping it for him.

Ryan caught the light with the razor and made several deep slices across his arm.

"Whoa, try one at a time. Savor them," she told him.

He savored them, the cuts, the ribbons of blood reflecting the candlelight. He savored his life dripping away in the darkness. Maybe his sacrifice would shock them, make them stop this destructive behavior. He hoped his story would outlive him.

He heard the screams as if in a dream.

The Interview

"Just get it, Kezia." Anna ordered. My hands shook and I twisted them together to hide it. My chest threatened to squeeze the air from my lungs. I glanced at the door to the basement. I could sprint up the stairs, across the street and be in my bedroom sanctuary with a good book in under a minute. And ruin any chance of having friends in high school, ever.

WWTSD? What would Taylor Swift do? I drew in a deep belly breath and a belch of pepperoni pizza popped out as I struggled to stand. Swear to God my knees did not knock together although Neon snickered. I glanced around at the three girls assessing me and made my choice. I knew where the Ouija board was because I buried it a few minutes ago under a pile of games after we did our nails on it. Mine were "Screaming Teal" and they matched Anna's. I didn't want to touch the stupid board when we *weren't* using it to summon something foul. Now it froze the blood in my veins.

I could do scary movies if the bad guys were, like, human or aliens that looked like humans. Giant, evil insects bent on Earth's destruction were disgusting but I could handle them. The supernatural stuff, not so much. My heritage was what screwed me up. I'm Gypsy on my dad's side. When he died two years ago, my mom took us away from the clan and plunked us into middle class suburbia. The gypsies were all, like, symbols and omens. They don't move a step without consulting some dead bug or something. Even though I knew it was all stupid, I still get those bad vibes, the heebie jeebies, around spooky stuff. My teeth clench and a hot steel ball races around my stomach until bile crawls up my throat and makes me want to yak.

In fact, I had puked during a late night babysitting gig this summer. I fell asleep on the Hagan's couch and when I snapped to, some black and white movie with Devil worship was in full black mass. Sour sweat sprang out of my pores, my stomach did an inward half gainer and I was up and running for the toilet. I harked up popcorn and Dr. Pepper with only a disgusted cat as my witness. Appropriate, since cats are the protectors of Gypsies.

Tonight was a turning point, an interview of sorts. These girls were seeing if they liked me enough to be friends. Being invited on a sleepover gave me five Awesome Points and I sure didn't want to lose them over some idiotic thing that could only last, how long? Twenty minutes? I could do this if I really had to.

I was jacked that Anna asked me: third week of high school, no less. I wasn't someone she hung with. OK, Truth: I didn't hang with anyone. Last week, everyone in bio laughed at the same time when their Snapchat went off except me and Diana, the Goth chick. She scrutinized her flat black hair for split ends but I decided right then I needed a plan. I needed a BFF: A Best Friend Forever seemed within my abilities and cheaper than a cell phone. I came up with the Awesome Point system. It's like Weight Watchers without the food.

I kept track of my points in a tiny notebook hidden in my pillowcase and I tried to be fair. The system seemed to be reaping me big benefits when I got invited to this sleepover.

I grabbed the board and was blinded! My sight was gone; everything went black. A shrill scream like tearing glass started and the lights snapped back on.

"Was that you, Kezia? I just turned off the lights," Anna was backed against the wall, hanging on the light switch like it was holding her up. Neon was in a defensive crouch, ready to fight and Marcy sat in the leather recliner glaring at me with enormous owl-eyes.

"Sorry," I mumbled, throwing the board to the carpet in front of Neon. She locked eyes with me as she lit a red candle with holly around it, some Christmas leftover with too much wax to toss. The heavy red drops joined and then pooled around the yellow wick.

"Lights are going off," Anna called out to no one in particular.

Neon's white blond hair reflected the light of the candle. It was buzzed on the sides so her scalp showed and one big thick lock hung over her face. Why couldn't I be more like her? She was fearless; a tiger in a tiny package.

She wore skirts so short you could almost see her butt cheeks and ripped black nylons. Hayden, the biggest jock in the school put his hand up her skirt in the lunchroom and she launched off her tiny feet and knocked him out with a right cross that would have made an MMA fighter smile. She didn't get in trouble for it either or not as much as you'd think. And you knew, just knew, she'd do it again if someone hassled her. I didn't envy her the Don't-Give-A-Rat's-Ass what you do parents, but maybe that was part of her gig.

Marcy completed our foursome. Marcy, plain as white yogurt but seriously smart. She could have been pretty but chose not to, IMHO. I mean, she had thick brown hair down her back and this heart shaped face with large blue eyes. A few highlights, some contacts and she would be gorgeous. She told us she was happier viewing the world through inch thick glasses that always had smudges on them.

My wavy hair is almost black, almost curly and not even close to tameable. It was really long until we left the clan and my mom had it cut. Now, it's stupid and makes like a halo around my head and I'm growing it out again, painful day by painful day. My eyes are really dark and my lashes are pretty good. Better if I was allowed to use mascara. I'm thin and my skin is dusky according to my mom and Mexican if you listen to jerks in the lunchroom, which I get tired of hearing. Same-O, Lame-O. My skin is pretty clear though and for that, I'm grateful. Zits on top of everything? Gag me.

I sat facing Neon, with Marcy on my right and Anna on my left. Please God, don't make us hold hands. Mine are wet and clammy. If I survive this, I'll do something good, I promise, like visit the old folk's home once a week, maybe. I like old people except for the smell; they're quiet inside somehow. Gypsies never send their Elders away from the family. I miss the Mamsa Jenkins, she smelled like jasmine and told fortunes. She always had time for me.

"Put your hands on the plastic thing," Anna whispered. I saw everyone else's painted nails already there and added my "Screaming Teal" to the mix.

"Is there a spirit out there? Come talk to us." Neon intoned.

I was swallowing like crazy but all the spit had left my mouth.

"Maybe we don't want anything to come," I whispered.

"It's the energy in our hands. Nothing is going to happen," Marcy's eyes rolled.

"If there is a spirit, make yourself known," Neon said.

I swear that plastic pointer thing moved. I didn't do it and Neon's mouth dropped open. Marcy's lips thinned into a line and Anna gasped.

N-O the pointer read.

"Ask it why not?" said Anna.

"Why won't you come, spirit?" Neon said.

The pointer moved quickly spelling H-E-R and stopped.

"Her. What does that mean?" Anna demanded.

"Sounds like it wants someone else to invite it," offered Marcy.

"I'll ask it," Anna said. "Is it me, spirit?"

The pointer didn't budge.

"Is it me, spirit?" Marcy spoke but no go. Shit.

"Kezia, ask it," whispered Neon.

Breathless, I mumbled, "Me?"

Y-E-S

Nervous giggles from the girls, blood in my mouth.

"Ask it why you?" said Anna, affronted.

The pointer slid. W-I-T-C-H.

"Cool, you're a witch," said Neon.

How does one react to this news with awesomeness? I was hard put to manage.

"Ask it if you have any powers," Neon said.

I didn't want any powers. I didn't want any more bile shooting up the back of my throat either but tonight was out of my hands.

"Do I have any powers?" I ventured. I'd seen the Avengers. Powers might be fun. I could hang with Loki who was rumored to be nice as well as sexy in his alter ego of Tom Hiddleston.

The light in the room rose like on a dimmer switch and holy shit, the hottest guy I've ever seen was standing just outside our circle. Looking at me. I clutched hands with the girls on either side of me. Just instinct, I guess and the smoldering man frowned. Motes of glitter floated around him, swirling as he moved.

"No need to fear me. I mean you no harm," his voice was like hot chocolate, smooth and tempting. "You invited me. Let's go somewhere we can talk, privately, like Paris." He smiled and held out a well shaped hand to me.

"No, I'm not leaving my friends." My heart pounded against my ribs like it was going to fly out.

"They aren't your friends, Kezia, not really. I can show you things, marvelous things. Give you access to powers, *chovani*." The Romani word for witch rolled out of his beautiful mouth and shivers marched up my back. "Help your mom so she doesn't have to work two jobs."

Images swirled around the room, glittering, shimmering. Me as I wanted to be: tall, slim, with boobs and a long dark cloud of hair. My mom relaxing and smiling at me. Famous people begging to be my friends. Somewhere, Anna's cat screamed and it all faded.

"No thanks," I said with a lot more confidence than I felt. Anna squeezed my hand. "What's the catch? What's the *bibaxt*?" It meant "bad luck" or "price" in Romanji.

He smirked and didn't look quite as cute as before. "You become one with me, after all is said and done and you've lived a full, glorious life."

"Exactly how does that happen?" The thing with demons, or so Mamsa Jenkins told me, was they couldn't lie if you asked them a direct question. The trick was, knowing the questions to ask.

He avoided my eyes. When he finally raised his head, I saw his bright blue eyes were glowing orange. "I eat your soul and any remaining body parts."

"Fuck," whispered Anna. All three pairs of eyes snapped to her. Anna never swore.

"Language!" Mocked Neon and we all giggled. Air came to me again. Anna's cat bumped into my back, hard. It broke my fascination with the slender, almost perfect being.

"Many have believed the journey worthy of the destination," he said. The cat swept across my back and then turned and nudged me with her other side. The only place I was warm was where the cat touched me. I began to focus on that warmth, like a lifeline.

"I'll keep these friends and my life," I told him and felt the cat purr against my back.

"We revoke our stupid invitation. Leave Kezia alone," Neon shouted.

"Yeah, she's our friend," Marcy added.

"And get out of my house, loser." Anna jumped up breaking our circle and hit the lights. I blinked once and wiped a hand across my damp eyes. I didn't care if they thought I was lame. I was way beyond caring. Neon put a bony arm across my shoulder and Anna handed me a tissue. The cat crawled into my lap and ran a rough tongue across my hand.

"Whoa. Look at that," Marcy pointed towards the basement door. Footprints impressions on the deep carpet, only just beginning to spring back as if from a great weight.

Also by Dixie Jo Jarchow

The Hunt for Mel's Gold
Hades' Redemption
Huntress Moon
The Gingerbread Man
Walking In the Graveyard

Watch for more at dixiejojarchow.com.

About the Author

Dixie Jo Jarchow writes in Black Wolf, WI with her husband and her two fearsome hounds.

Read more at www.dixiejojarchow.com.